The Seventh Sister

MILLIE ABECASSIS

ANUCI PRESS

This is a work of fiction. Names, characters, places, and incidents either are the product of the author's imagination or are used fictitiously. Any resemblance to actual persons, living or dead, events, or locales is entirely coincidental.

Copyright © 2026 by Millie Abecassis

All rights reserved. No part of this book may be reproduced or used in any manner without written permission of the copyright owner except for the use of quotations in a book review. For more information, address:

Tanuci69@gmail.com

First paperback edition 2026

Anuci Press edition 2026

www.anuci-press.com

Cover Design by Adrian Medina

fabledbeastdesign.com

Edited by Robert Ottone

ISBN 979-8-9989778-6-2 (paperback)

ISBN 979-8-9989778-7-9(eBook)

Also By Millie Abecassis

Daughters of the Blue Moon (Anuci Press, February 2025)
Bright City, Shattered (Polymath Press, June 2025)
***A* Legacy of Blood and Bone** (Brick & Bloom, October 2025)

Prologue

SHIZELLE

You were always a sister to me.

Even when I tried to kill you.

I like to think I was a sister to you, too. After all, only the two of us made it from the orphanage to the temple. All we had was each other. Two orphans who grew up in the same place with the same hopes and dreams and the feeling of not belonging anywhere. Without you, I wouldn't have survived the years of training they forced upon us. Oh, I could always leave, and so could you. But where would we go without family? What fate would have befallen us, two pesky adolescents barely old enough to drink the sun-ale made by nuns only three years our senior?

So, we stayed at the temple, and my sister you remained, even when I drew a dagger at your throat, ready to slice it to save my skin. If I hadn't failed miserably at my duty, I would have lost a sister. Worse, I would have prevented you from becoming a sister to others—and *that* would have been a catastrophe not only to myself, but to the entire world.

Sometimes, failure is a blessing.

Chapter One

ÉLIANE

"And now, look at him," the High Seer said to Éliane, pointing at Aurië, the Sun-God, in the sky.

Éliane exhaled, gathering her strength. This was the moment she had been preparing for. Five years of training at the temple as a nun, reading about the divine astral being hovering above all in the sky, learning his ways, memorizing rituals, preparing sun-ale alongside the other nuns under the gaze of seers whose eyes let them see beyond the material world.

Blinking, Éliane readied herself for the discomfort that awaited her eyes. It was time to rise from nun to seer, no matter how difficult the ritual was. Only by looking directly at the sun would she gain true sight. All the seers gathered for the occasion had been through the same ritual, and the other nuns would do the same once they were ready.

I am ready.

Opening her eyes, she lifted her head slowly until her gaze met Aurië. She looked away immediately, her instincts telling her to safeguard her sight by avoiding the god's burning light. But her instincts were wrong. She wouldn't go blind. Her training at the temple had prepared her body and soul to confront Aurië's light, so it could gift her with true sight instead of taking it away.

So, she looked again, and this time she resisted the urge to avert her eyes or close them.

"The sightening has begun," the High Seer said. "Keep embracing his light, Éliane. You know it won't hurt you."

It didn't hurt indeed, despite the constant temptation to look away. As expected, Aurië's light was intense and difficult to bear, but it wasn't blinding. Éliane's retina welcomed the induced transformation, aptly prepared to change and not burn. Had she undergone the sightening without being a nun, she would have forfeited her vision for eternal darkness—an eternal darkness Aurië had fought hard himself, putting an end to the terror of Nunia, the Night-Goddess. He wouldn't allow himself to cast earthly creatures in the dark by blinding them. If Nunia had used the absence of light to reach her goal, Aurië knew that too much of it caused the same outcome and had provided the men and women serving him with the means to welcome his light and his gifts without succumbing to darkness.

As she kept watching the sun, Éliane remembered how she prepared herself for this moment. The endless prayers, the sleepless nights. The drops in her eyes, the sun-ale in her mouth. The sun-water vapor filling her lungs, the concoctions hurting her stomach. A path she didn't choose, but that chose her—and chose wisely, for she didn't suffer the training side effects as harshly as her companions, as if her body was naturally more inclined to accept Aurië's gifts.

On bended knees, her eyes solely focused on the divine star who made life possible on Ido, the Earth-God on which Éliane lived, she lost track of time. The High Seer's voice commanded her to look longer, and longer, and longer again, until the sun was so low on the horizon that the ritual came to a natural conclusion. Finally, an end to this hours-long ordeal. *I did it*, Éliane thought. *I did it and won't have to do it again.*

"The sightening is over," the High Seer concluded, ordering Éliane to rise. "You have successfully stared at Aurië for a half-day, gaining the gifts he bestows to his most loyal followers. Rise, Seer Éliane, for you are one of us."

Éliane stood up with difficulty, her legs numbed by the hours spent on the cold stones paving the temple's western courtyard. She wasn't blind, but her vision was blurry. Only a temporary effect of the sightening ritual. She could still distinguish the silhouettes of the people in attendance. The other nuns of her age who would soon undergo the sightening themselves, only a half-dozen of them. Dame Héloïse, the godkin acting as the temple's counselor, who climbed down her tower to witness the making of another of her divine father's servants. The temple's guards, among them her friend Shizelle, the youngest and brightest of them. And of course, seers. Too many for Éliane to count them, even if her vision were crystal-clear.

The High Seer put her hand on Éliane's back and pushed her gently toward the temple's doors. "You will spend the night in the recovering room, in total darkness, so your eyes can rest."

Éliane didn't want to spend the night in the recovery room. A burning curiosity filled her mind, telling her to try *seeing* like a seer now. The preparations had taken so many years! Why couldn't she use her new abilities immediately? But she knew why, and she didn't argue with the High Seer. Not only did she need rest, but her pupils' transformation would only be complete after a night in darkness.

"Tomorrow," the High Seer said, "your real work begins."

Chapter Two

ÉLIANE

In the recovery room, a dreamless sleep overtook Éliane the moment she slipped under the blankets. Nobody came for her, and without any window for the sunlight to wake her up naturally, she slept until late morning for the first time in five years.

Opening her eyes scared her. What if the ritual hadn't worked, and her retina was damaged beyond repair? What if she missed a step in her training, forgot to drink one of the sour floral concoctions sharpening her senses, or the right amount of sun-ale to open her body and mind to Aurië, or—*no*, she told herself, exhaling. It was fear talking. Irrational fear, as always. The High Seer would have never let her undergo the sightening ritual if she hadn't deemed her apt to do so. She knew when a nun was ready.

When Éliane resolved herself to look around, only darkness greeted her. At least, neither her cornea nor her eyelids hurt. A good sign. Now, she needed to get out of the recovery room to finally test her new abilities and confirm she could still see—and see *more* than before.

"I was expecting you to come out later," the High Seer said when Éliane pushed the door open. She sat in a velvet armchair right next to the door, a book on her lap. This observation made Éliane realize she could still see. The sightening had worked. But this wasn't it. A veil now covered her gaze. A new layer of reality revealed itself to her.

According to her training, this was how she could now see shades. Éliane couldn't see any shade around the High Seer, but it didn't mean none existed. As a seer, and as the best one in the temple, the High Seer could conceal her own shades. For all Éliane knew, a dark cloud of grief or sadness or guilt or any other negative emotion could follow the High Seer, yet she would never see it unless she surpassed the woman in skill.

"I never slept that long," Éliane said at last, collecting herself.

"I slept almost twenty-four hours straight after my own sightening," the High Seer said, shrugging. "You are an early riser, by sightening norms. But it's a good thing," she added before Éliane had a chance to ask. "This means you can practice your first glimpsing ritual today."

Éliane nodded, half-apprehensive, half-excited. Seeing shades didn't require a ritual, only focus and practice. Glimpsings, however, were a different matter. She studied the theory extensively, but it didn't mean her first glimpsing would be successful. Most seers didn't catch glimpses of possible futures for weeks, sometimes months or years.

Expecting the same experience, Éliane followed the High Seer to the glimpsing hall. The room was the largest in the temple. In its center stood a stone fountain depicting Aurië in his corporeal form—a man with long hair most people described as both impressive and charming—pouring water into a fountain from a jar. With the incense burning in the thuribles hanging from the ceiling, the flow of the water gave the glimpsing hall a relaxing atmosphere, helping the seers who busied themselves with the ritual Éliane was about to practice and fail. Their tranced eyes were of that pale, translucent yellow that replaced whatever color they were born with. She hadn't seen her reflection since her sightening, but Éliane knew her own eyes looked the same now. The seers all sat in front of a worshipper whose future they attempted to glimpse at. People came from distant towns and cities to consult with one of Aurië's seers against a modest donation to the temple. Éliane wondered who came for her today, and already felt sorry for them. She wouldn't be able to give them a clear—or even blurry—view of what possibility awaited them in the next days or weeks.

"Let's sit next to Seer Ahma," the High Seer said, gesturing at the man, who sat cross-legged on a green mat, visibly lost into a particularly long glimpse—a full-fledged vision, at this point. In front of him was another man—the worshipper Seer Ahma tended to today—looking at him apprehensively as if he knew his future was going to be terrible. If only people understood what seers glimpsed at was only a *possibility*. The most likely future, yes, but it could still change.

Éliane did as she was told, glancing at Seer Ahma with that curiosity of hers she struggled to control. He was one of the oldest seers and the High Seer's right hand, running the temple in her absence. He had taught Éliane many times, yet she had never seen him during a glimpsing ritual. Did he leave the quietness of his private office, where he usually received worshippers, for the crowded glimpsing hall to witness her practice today?

Gulping with unease, Éliane shook her head to chase away the anxiety-inducing thoughts. Nobody expected her to succeed today. There was no point in putting pressure on herself. She would give the ritual a try, fail, learn from her failure, try again, fail more, and do it all over again until her mind finally interpreted the signals sent by her changed eyes.

"Who am I seeing today?" Éliane asked, glancing at the crowd of worshippers waiting in line at the entrance of the glimpsing hall.

"Nobody."

Éliane cocked her head in surprise. Seers could only glimpse at the future of regular people. They couldn't glimpse at their own future or at another seer's. Aurië gifted them with true sight so they could help common folks. She couldn't practice without a worshipper. Though, Éliane remembered, it wasn't entirely true. Seers could also glimpse at the possible futures of the place they were in. That, minus themselves or other seers present in said place, of course.

"For your first glimpsing attempt, I want you to focus on the temple."

Éliane found it curious. Any glimpsing in the temple wouldn't be interesting, since it was mostly inhabited by seers. But she didn't object to the High Seer's request. Perhaps none of the worshippers present today had agreed to volunteer to train a new seer. After all, people who came to the temple wanted answers, and she wouldn't have any for them.

Following the High Seer's guidance, she recited the prayer to Aurië she knew by heart, except this time it should induce a glimpsing. The prayer over, she brought to her lips the cup of sun-ale the High Seer had just poured for her, and let the sweet golden beverage warm her mouth and body like a pleasant late-afternoon ray of sunshine.

Immediately, she found herself gazing at scenes taking place before her eyes, as if she was in another place and another time. She was still on the mat in the glimpsing hall, she knew, but her vision was saturated with an unending succession of images. Nothing made sense. Flashes of reds and yellows and greens and blues and light and darkness blended together, masking the faces of the people she saw, bleeding into the landscape of the locations they were in, and making the glimpsings impossible to interpret. But she was *glimpsing*, at least. It was better than expected.

Éliane drank another gulp of sun-ale, hoping it would clear her vision—and it did, if only for an instant. The blend of colors suddenly became clear, letting her glimpse at Dame Héloïse's face, in her tower. Éliane didn't hear what she said—a glimpsing was a *glimpsing*, not a hearing—but the woman seemed concerned. Was something bad going to happen at the temple?

Before Éliane could ask herself more questions, the glimpsing vanished as quickly as it had appeared, and she blurted, "I glimpsed at the future."

"Did you?" Seer Ahma asked, a smile on his face. The worshipper in front of him was gone. How long did Éliane spend glimpsing? Probably more time that it had felt.

The High Seer frowned, observing Éliane. Then she shook her head and declared, "Impossible."

"I felt it," Seer Ahma argued. "Didn't you?"

"I did indeed," the High Seer admitted reluctantly, her voice taut. "What did you see, Seer Éliane?"

Éliane gulped, sensing the High Seer's tension not only in her voice but also in the sharp look she gave her, which sent a shiver down her spine. She had never seen the High Seer unhappy. Unsatisfied. What did she do to deserve her superior's ire? Clearing her throat, Éliane said, "I saw Dame Héloïse in her tower. She seemed..."—she paused, choosing her words carefully—"...concerned."

More seers approached the yellow mat where she and the High Seer sat. Their whispers rose in the air, adding to the worry already compressing Éliane's chest. Some looked incredulous, while others were visibly joyful—the emotion Éliane should be feeling now, having accomplished what the High Seer deemed impossible. But her superior's reaction had immediately extinguished the ounce of excitement Éliane had felt after her unprecedented success. Did the High Seer have good reasons to be so tense? Was it dangerous for Éliane's eyes and mind to progress too fast?

"Remarkable," the High Seer said, her voice flat and icy, "but it could only be beginner's luck. We shall see if you can reproduce today's experience tomorrow. For now, it's best to let your body rest after not one, but *two* incredible experiences. A sightening *and* a glimpsing back-to-back are certain to exhaust you."

I don't feel tired, she wanted to tell the High Seer, but she knew better than to contradict her superior's decisions, especially after her unexpected negative reaction. Éliane wished she could see the High Seer's shades, to put a word on what emotions the woman felt, but it was, despite her recent success, out of her reach. For how long, she wondered? Did today's success forecast a fast progression, to the point that she would equal or even surpass the High Seer soon enough? Or was it mere delusion filling her mind? Perhaps it was beginner's luck, after all. The only way to know was to try again tomorrow, and tomorrow, and the days after.

***

It wasn't beginner's luck.

As soon as the worshippers heard Éliane was *good*, they lined up to see her. She kept glimpsing each day she practiced the ritual, seeing fragments of people's possible futures with more and more ease, from predicting a healthy birth to an expectant mother, to a poor harvest to a farmer who had neglected his fields. Her glimpses often reassured, sometimes scared. At least they allowed people to adjust the course of their lives to avoid the worst.

The High Seer couldn't hide her emotions anymore, and soon Seer Ahma questioned her about the anger-shaped shade following her around, confirming what Éliane suspected. Unsurprisingly, the High Seer dismissed the question and retreated to her office, leaving Éliane under the man's care.

"She'll get over it," he told Éliane with a reassuring voice that failed to reassure her. It wasn't his fault; Éliane's anxiety was simply too high to disappear with mere words. "The High Seer can become irritable when things don't go according to her plans, but she'll get over it. She always does."

What's the High Seer's plan? Éliane wondered. And how her faster-than-expected progress worked against it? Regardless, she had done nothing wrong. She had never asked to progress faster than normal. The High Seer misdirected her anger and caused Éliane unfair distress.

Seer Ahma put his hand on her shoulder. "She'll get over it."

Éliane soon found out Seer Ahma wasn't wrong—though she hesitated to deem his judgment *right*. After a few days, the High Seer didn't look angry anymore. Nobody asked her about shades after that one time she failed at hiding them from other seers. But her lips remained pursed and her face cold, as if a mild-but-persistent *annoyance* replaced the now-gone anger. Despite her anxious thoughts, Éliane didn't let it distract her practice. There were plenty of other seers like Ahma willing to help her, and even more willing to praise her rapid progress. She did her best to focus on these.

"Aurië's worshippers are pleased by your ability to glimpse at their possible futures so easily," one seer said. "They keep asking for you."

"Less work for us," many added, blinking at her, "and more time for prayer."

"Such prowess is unheard of," another said. "The Sun-God must have blessed you personally during your sightening to reward your piety."

Éliane welcomed their compliments with polite nods and humbleness. She hadn't been blessed by Aurië—he would have spoken to her during the sightening, and he didn't. Mere chance granted her the natural capacity to perform better and faster than other seers. She was born this way, it appeared. Nothing she could be proud of. She wasn't more pious or studious than them.

"Chance or not, we're glad to have you."

It was a pleasant change, at least. Éliane hadn't succeeded in forming friendships with other nuns studying Aurië's ways—even with Talya, another nun a year her junior often assigned to sun-ale duty alongside her. She had made acquaintances at best, rivals at worst, and had feared for a while that the seers would treat her worse than her then-fellow apprentices. Only Shizelle was there for her, as she had always been since they met each other at the orphanage.

"I'm surprised they aren't jealous," Shizelle told her one day that they were strolling alongside the northern wall, to avoid the line of querying worshippers already forming at the southern entrance. "Though the High Seer obviously is."

"She'll get over it," Éliane said, repeating Seer Ahma's words like a hopeful mantra. She was trying to convince herself more than Shizelle.

"What if she doesn't?"

Éliane smiled and said, taking Shizelle's hand affectionately, "Then you'll protect me like you protect the temple."

Chapter Three

ÉLIANE, BEFORE

"Get up, girls!" Mrs. Breval, the orphanage director, said in a hurried tone. "The High Seer is visiting today to pick two of you for her temple. Come on, faster! She won't come back for a while, so if you want a chance to be selected, it's now or never."

Éliane grumbled under the bedsheets, but she knew not to test Mrs. Breval's patience. Around her, the other adolescents were getting up and changing into their day clothes, and soon she imitated them. In truth, she was excited. As soon as Mrs. Breval told them about the High Seer's forthcoming visit, she had been curious to meet the woman. Seers had yellow eyes, something she had never seen. It sounded so unreal. She wanted to see it to believe it. If only it wasn't so early in the morning!

"I'm sure she'll choose the prettiest," Shizelle told Éliane as they walked outside of the dormitory. "Like Clémence, or Enya."

Éliane shrugged. "I don't know. Seers don't need to be pretty."

"I just hope they don't pick me."

"Why not?" Éliane asked. They both only had one year before the orphanage would kick them out to fend for themselves. The orphans who approached their seventeenth birthday coveted any opportunity to leave with a stable future, Éliane among them.

"I don't want to leave without you," Shizelle whispered, filling Éliane's heart with affection.

She squeezed her friend's hand as they lined up in front of Mrs. Breval in the communal room. Shizelle had joined the orphanage after Éliane, when she was already six and had lost her family in a fire, while Éliane was almost born there. Both still had living family, but none that could or would take care of them. Shizelle, because her aunt was a poor widow who couldn't afford one more mouth to feed, and Éliane, because nobody wanted to raise a child born out of wedlock from an unknown father, whose very birth had caused her mother's death. Éliane immediately noticed the sadness in the new girl's look, and instead of joining the other girls teasing Shizelle for not being as pretty as they thought she should be, she befriended her. When they reached puberty, Shizelle grew up taller than everyone else—Mrs. Breval included—and the teasing stopped as abruptly as it began. It was Shizelle's turn to shield Éliane from the teasing, looking dead in the eye whoever dared mocking her for being too small and too thin and too shy and too many not-enough things.

Éliane didn't want Shizelle to leave either, but what she hadn't anticipated was that *she* would be the one leaving her friend behind.

"You," the High Seer said, approaching her, "what is your name?"

"This is Éliane," Mrs. Breval said. "She is—"

"I asked *her*, not you," the High Seer snapped. But instead of asking Éliane to repeat what Mrs. Breval had just said, she turned to her and asked, "You know Aurië, is that right?"

Éliane froze, stricken by both the question and the High Seer's eyes, who truly were yellow, almost like gold. What did it take for a seer to get such pupils? Was it painful? Again, her curious mind couldn't help but *wonder*, and the anxious side of her thought about pain and hardship. But now wasn't the time to let her mind wander. The High Seer was waiting.

Éliane nodded, answering silently the woman's question. She could have lied, so the High Seer would lose interest in her, but everyone knew about the gods and goddesses surrounding them, from the one they walked on—Ido, the Earth-God—to the ones in the skies like Aurië. Lying would have been vain. The High Seer's question was purely performative, a way to discuss directly with Éliane and tell Mrs. Breval to remain quiet.

"Do you love him?"

What an odd question! Who didn't like the sun? Its warmth made life possible, its light chased the darkness, its beauty brightened the sky. The High Seer could have asked Éliane if she enjoyed breathing that Éliane would have been surprised all the same.

When she realized the High Seer actually expected an answer, Éliane stuttered, "I-I do."

"I can feel it," the High Seer said, staring at Éliane with these eerie eyes of hers. "I believe you'd make a fine seer, after your nunship. What do you say?"

The High Seer was inviting Éliane to leave the place she called home, but a home that had never loved her except for Shizelle. Of course, she wanted to leave. Becoming a seer was a prestigious future, one few orphans could pretend to, for the High Seer only visited orphanages when noble families failed to produce enough children so they could spare the youngest to Aurië. But she didn't want to leave without Shizelle, no more than Shizelle wanted to leave without her.

Gathering her courage, she cleared her throat to ready her voice and said, "It would be an honor to serve Aurië, but I would like my friend Shizelle to come with me."

Whispers rose in the air from girls who, according to what Éliane heard, found it unfair for Éliane to choose who would be the second orphan to join the temple. Éliane didn't disagree with them, but none of these girls had been kind to Shizelle nor to herself, and if she didn't wish them harm, she didn't feel bad for asking the High Seer a favor. She had to try to take her friend with her.

"Silence," Mrs. Breval said before apologizing to the High Seer for the girls' behavior.

The High Seer ignored Mrs. Breval and the whispering adolescents and cast a curious look at Shizelle, as if she was reading her very soul. Could seers do such a thing, Éliane wondered? The woman's yellow eyes were immobile, unblinking, riveted on Shizelle who wasn't moving, her whole body seemingly frozen in place either by fear or by a supernatural force.

"She won't make a good seer," the High Seer said at last, her judgment followed by a flurry of relieved sighs from the other girls. "But," she added before Éliane or Shizelle had a chance to insist, "she could make a good guard. Tall, athletic"—she grabbed Shizelle's face and opened her mouth, inspecting her teeth—"good health. She will do."

Shizelle winced and rubbed her hand against her mouth after the High Seer released her grasp. Her eyes burned with the anger of having been inspected like cattle, but Éliane knew her friend was smart enough not to object, if she wanted to follow Éliane.

"But I warn you, girl—"

"My name is Shizelle," she said with a hint of insolence Éliane didn't fail to catch, but that didn't seem to bother the High Seer if she heard it.

"I warn you, *Shizelle*. It won't be easy. You'll train hard among men. They won't show you any mercy if you can't keep up with them, and I won't either. The temple possesses many treasures, and not only made of gold." She pointed at Éliane. "Our nuns and seers are our greatest treasure; one our enemies covet relentlessly. If you can't protect yourself, then you can't protect her. Can you protect yourself?"

"I very well can," Shizelle said between her teeth, her eyes locked on the High Seer's in that defiant way Éliane had seen her cast at the orphanage's girls so many times.

"Good." The High Seer turned to Mrs. Breval. "I have what I came for."

"But..." a voice said hesitantly—Enya, Éliane recognized, "you came for two seers, and you only have one."

"I came for two *girls*," the High Seer said coldly, before turning around and walking toward the temple's exit.

Éliane gave a half-questioning, half-panicked look at Shizelle. Were they supposed to leave now? Shizelle gave her the same look before saying, "What about our things?"

The High Seer stopped at the door, sighed, and said, looking at Mrs. Breval, "Would you kindly arrange for their belongings to be transferred to the temple? Only the strict necessary."

Shizelle grabbed Éliane's hand and led her toward the High Seer. Éliane stumbled behind her, too stunned to realize what was happening. She was leaving the orphanage forever, and she was leaving with Shizelle. How was it possible? Why her? She had never been keen on worshipping the gods, should it be Aurië or the others. What did the High Seer see in her? She was just an average orphan girl who couldn't read and who had never stepped into a temple.

"You will learn," the High Seer told her, as if she had heard her thoughts.

Éliane squeezed Shizelle's hand, and without looking back, she followed the High Seer to her new home.

Chapter Four

THE HIGH SEER

How dare she? That girl that *she* had saved from the orphanage, from a life of misery. How dare she cast a shadow on her savior barely after becoming a seer?

The High Seer gritted her teeth as she climbed the stairs leading to the home of Dame Héloïse, silently cursing herself for letting her emotions run so high that she lost focus and let others see her shades. It never happened before. Not since she had risen to her current rank, the highest in the temple, surpassed only by She-Who-Sees-All, the forever servant of Aurië living in the largest temple in the capital.

"You look troubled," Dame Héloïse said when she opened the door leading to her home, a unique room that overlooked the temple and the surrounding region. "I don't need to be able to see your shades to know it."

Dame Héloïse was a godkin of Aurië—a child of the Sun-God and of a human mother—and had never undergone the sightening. She wasn't a seer, but her divine father had still gifted her with inner light and warmth that she could cast at will, chasing the darkness away as if she was a star in the middle of the night.

"I've been boiling with anger for the past weeks and it's killing me," the High Seer said, walking inside. "I don't know what to do anymore."

"Why don't you start by drinking some sun-ale with me?" Dame Héloïse offered, pointing at the table and chairs in the middle of the large circular room. "I made this batch myself with the light my father gave me."

Exhaling, the High Seer nodded and sat at the table. Outside, Aurië hid behind large clouds, which was unusual for this time of the year. The High Seer couldn't help but compare it with her own situation. Éliane was like one of these clouds, coming too early for the season and casting a shadow on the High Seer before her time had come.

"Tell me, Héloïse. Who is the brightest seer in the temple?"

Dame Héloïse chuckled as she put the sun-ale mugs on the table. "Is it really the advice you came seeking today?"

"It is."

"You are indeed deeply troubled, if you are asking yourself this question—for the answer is obvious."

"I don't believe it is anymore, and that's the issue."

"You *are* the brightest seer in the temple, you idiot," Dame Héloïse said, a smile at the corner of her lips.

If anybody else had been talking, the High Seer would have unleashed her fury on them, but Dame Héloïse wasn't anybody. She was an old friend, and she had called the High Seer an idiot more than once. Her long life—longer than the average human because of her godkin nature—and the experience coming with it gave her the right to tell High Seers when they behaved like fools, and today was no exception.

Normally, Dame Héloïse's wise words were enough to soothe the High Seer and alleviate her doubts, but normalcy left her mind weeks ago, when Éliane had glimpsed at possible futures on her first attempt. The more she thought about it, the more it infuriated her. It wasn't normal. It wasn't how things were supposed to happen. She had always planned to select a successor, but only when the time came. What happened with Éliane wasn't mere luck, as the girl claimed. It was heresy.

"What about Éliane?" she asked at last, sipping her sun-ale. There was no point in lying to Dame Héloïse about the source of her concerns.

"Éliane... she's very bright, too."

"Brighter than me?"

"Not yet, but she will soon be as bright as you. And not long after, she will surpass you. I don't need to glimpse at the future to know it. Everyone has noticed her abilities, myself included."

"What of me, then?" the High Seer exclaimed uncontrollably. "If she surpasses me, everyone will expect me to retire early and name her my successor. I'll have to join She-Who-Sees-All's court and will be ridiculed for doing so at such a young age. I won't survive my first winter before shadows overtake me."

"It doesn't have to be this way."

"It *will*, and you know it, Héloïse. Please don't lie to me."

"I would never." Dame Héloïse gulped her sun-ale down and added, "Why don't you send her on a pilgrimage? I know it's early... but everything is early about this girl. It would do you some good. She would be away for some time, giving you the opportunity to calm down and refocus on your priority—the temple. Hopefully, when she comes back, you will be in a better mindset, and meanwhile we will work together on a plan that will not compromise the girl's future or yours."

The High Seer's eyes opened wide. Sending Éliane away. It was brilliant. Why didn't she think of it herself? Dame Héloïse's presence was truly a blessing. Smiling for the first time in weeks, she said, "What would I do without your advice, Héloïse? I shall do exactly that."

As she walked down the tower, her stomach full with sun-ale and a smirk on her face, the High Seer considered her next steps. She would send Éliane on a pilgrimage.

But she won't come back.

Chapter Five

ÉLIANE

"Let her come in," the voice of the High Seer said from inside her office.

A guard opened the door for Éliane and gave her a curt nod. Inside, the High Seer sat at her desk, writing in a bulky ledger, her brows furrowed. After long seconds of uncomfortable silence, she put her quill down and said, a tight-lipped smile on her face, "Sit."

Éliane did as she was told, ignoring the discomfort rising inside her chest. When the High Seer summoned someone in her office, it was rarely for something other than a sermon. Considering the High Seer's recent attitude toward her, Éliane had no reason to believe she was here for a cup of tea.

"You asked for me," she said softly, not wanting to upset the High Seer more than she seemed to be.

"I did indeed, and there you are. This won't be long." The High Seer put away her ledger and clasped her hands. Casting an intense look at Éliane, she said, "You are going to Fahein."

Éliane blinked. The High Seer wanted her to go to the capital? There was only one reason for seers to travel there, and it was for their pilgrimage. A pilgrimage she didn't expect to accomplish before at least five years.

"You heard me very well," the High Seer said, reading in Éliane's mind like an open book. "You will pay homage to She-Who-Sees-All and receive her benediction. You're ready."

It's absurd, Éliane told herself. True, she progressed faster than anyone else, and her glimpses gained in length and precision every day, but the pilgrimage wasn't a mere reward for glimpsing excellence. It was a path of faith and devotion to Aurië, and if she had learned all the prayers and acts of devotions like other nuns, she had been communing with the Sun-God as a seer for less than two months.

No, the High Seer didn't think she was ready. She had another motive.

"You want to send me away," Éliane said, barely concealing the bitterness in her voice. "Why?"

"This isn't up for discussion," the High Seer said sharply, confirming Éliane's intuition. "You're leaving tomorrow morning, so you'll be back before winter."

Éliane wanted to argue, but she knew better than to challenge a direct order from her superior, especially in front of a witness. A guard stood by the door, a guard the High Seer could order to escort Éliane to the underground cells filled with captured assailants and deviant seers. She was way too scared of ending down there to open her mouth.

So instead, she took a deep breath in to calm her hammering heart. Éliane had never intended to be so good at glimpsing. She had never wanted to progress so quickly. A regular pace would have satisfied her. But the High Seer couldn't understand it, no matter how many times Éliane bowed and diverted the compliments and acted with modesty.

There was no other way but to do what her superior wanted. Éliane gritted her teeth as the sour taste of resentment filled her mouth. The High Seer was so pointlessly jealous that she wanted to send her away on a lengthy pilgrimage? Fine. She would go, and she would submit to She-Who-Sees-All's scrutiny. She would pass the test of faith and come back blessed, her aura brighter than ever. Then the High Seer would have a proper reason to complain about the shadow she believed Éliane cast on her.

"I should get my things ready then," she simply said.

"Yes, you should," the High Seer answered, folding her arms. "Don't forget to pack sun-shells. It can get dangerous on the road."

She said it with a smirk on her face, as if she hoped Éliane would get in trouble during her pilgrimage. It didn't matter. Éliane had listened well enough during her lessons to know how to act during a pilgrimage. Always stick to the road, don't carry anything of value, wear the yellow robe of pilgrims to showcase your status—and yes, take sun-shells with you in case you needed to repeal a wild creature or scare scoundrels bothering you. Nothing she couldn't handle.

She didn't speak, didn't bow to the High Seer as protocol required, and walked out of her superior's office under the gaze of the guard, who could barely contain his own surprise. Éliane was surprised at her own audacity too, but she needed it to make it to Fahein. It was time to borrow a bit of Shizelle's courage.

***

The next day, her backpack ready and her yellow pilgrim robe on, she went to the glimpsing hall to say goodbye to the seers who had become her friends during the last few weeks. Seer Ahma was the most troubled of all, but also the most supportive.

"You will make it. It's only three weeks away. Stay on the trail. Always keep a sun-shell in your pocket, ready for use. The inns will feed and lodge you for free against offering a glimpsing or two to their customers, so don't be shy."

A faint smile on her face, Éliane nodded while she listened to his advice, but her mind was somewhere else. Shizelle wasn't here. Not in the glimpsing hall, not near the main gate. Why didn't she come to say goodbye? They wouldn't see each other for at least two months. Was she upset at Éliane's decision not to challenge the High Seer's order? Or was she too sad and wanted to avoid crying in public? Shizelle had learned the hard way to hide her emotions. She couldn't have become a guard if she had allowed others to see what they considered a weakness, and if Éliane regretted how cold her friend had become, she understood. Her heart still clenching with disappointment, she left the safety of the temple for the long mountainous hike awaiting her.

To join the trail, she first walked to Howe, the closest village, where she also requested donations for her pilgrimage on the main square. Faithful to the tradition, the villagers responded with grace and offered her dried meats and fruits and cheeses and words of encouragement. They didn't fail to notice her unusual youth for a pilgrim, and offered to pray Aurië for a safe trip to the capital. She thanked them all and departed the village shortly after midday, hoping to join the first inn indicated on her map by sundown.

It took her less than an hour to reach the beginning of the trail. Its tortuous, dusty road led deep inside the woods, Éliane knew, and she didn't look forward to the ascending part. At least she would have a comfortable bed to sleep in once she reached the inn. This wouldn't always be the case. Some nights, she would have to sleep in the small tent she carried in her backpack, praying to the Sun-God to protect her from curious bears and hungry wolves. Looking up at Aurië, who was high in the sky, she whispered a brief prayer and began her pilgrimage.

Solitude was her sole companion, but not for long. As she reached the edge of the forest, she heard rushed footsteps behind her. She stopped and glanced nervously over her shoulder. Nobody was there. Could have she mistaken the running of a wild animal for someone's steps? Yes, this must be it—though it wasn't reassuring. Deer and boars filled the woods, and if she didn't mind encountering the former, she needed to avoid the latter.

Squeezing the sun-shell in her right pocket, Éliane ventured farther into the woods, careful not to leave the trail. She knew she should make noise to scare the wildlife away, but the not-footsteps had startled her. Now she moved silently, careful not to step on branches, as if the quietest sound would reveal her position to some secret follower. This was silly, she told herself, but her body couldn't help but move carefully on the trail. If she could see her own shades, a fear-shaped one would surely be looming over her.

The sound of crackling dead leaves made her freeze. It didn't come from behind her this time, but from her right. Slowly, she looked in that direction and almost gasped when a figure emerged from between the trees. If she hadn't immediately recognized Shizelle, her heart would have exploded. What was she doing here? Did she regret missing her chance to say goodbye in the morning, and had run after her to apologize and hug her one last time?

"You almost gave me a heart attack."

Shizelle didn't respond. Instead, she moved toward Éliane, her face stern and her fists clenched as if she was ready to punch something—or *someone*, Éliane caught herself thinking. But Shizelle was her friend. She swore to protect her. Shizelle must have spotted a threat and was readying herself to fight it. The thought made Éliane look around to find whatever caused Shizelle's alertness, but she couldn't see anything among the trees or on the trail.

They were alone.

When she glanced back at Shizelle with a questioning look, Éliane's heart sank in a well of darkness, as if Aurië would never shine on her anymore. A shade hovered above Shizelle, its shape unclear, but betraying her somber intent. She held a dagger in her left hand and a dark blue sphere in her right. A night-shell to counteract the effect of the sun-shell Éliane now considered throwing at the woman she thought to be her friend.

As Shizelle moved toward her, a dark, menacing look on her face, Éliane said pressingly, "What are you doing?"

Shizelle remained silent, her eyes riveted to Éliane's throat, as if she already saw herself slicing it. *This can't be happening*, Éliane thought. Something or someone had to be controlling her friend's actions. Perhaps a godkin of Nunia still roaming the earth, longing for the return of their dead divine mother, who had seized the opportunity to slaughter a disciple of Nunia's fiercest enemy. But... why choose Shizelle for such a task? They couldn't have entered the temple. Shizelle and other guards would have killed them before they had a chance to approach the walls.

"You don't have to do this," Éliane said, carefully stepping backward. "Speak to me, Shizelle."

Shizelle didn't stop moving menacingly toward Éliane, her lips pressed against each other. Éliane had no choice. She had to run. The sun-shell would injure Shizelle, and despite the situation, she didn't want to hurt her. That was if she managed to throw it before Shizelle used her night-shell, nullifying the sun-shell's blinding, burning light. A night-shell, Éliane suddenly realized, that Shizelle must have obtained at the temple from the only person allowed to craft and dispense them.

The High Seer.

"She sent you to kill me?" Éliane said, half-stunned, half-incredulous. "Of all people, she sent *you*?" If this wasn't cruelty, she didn't know what was.

The shade above Shizelle's head morphed into one of anger, and she dashed forward, hitting Éliane with full force before she had a chance to flee. Éliane used all her strength to push Shizelle away, but her friend was too tall, too strong, and soon she found herself lying on the ground with a dagger against her throat, unable to move.

"Shizelle," she pleaded, wincing at the coldness of the blade against her skin. "Please."

Her friend stared at her for long, dreadful seconds. Her jaw was locked and her hand gripping the dagger, pressing it dangerously against Éliane's throat, but unmoving. What was she waiting for? Was she finally coming back to her senses, or about to end Éliane's life because the High Seer ordered it?

"I can't," Shizelle finally said before throwing her dagger away and letting out a cry of anger. She rolled to the side, freeing Éliane from her clutch.

Silence followed, only disturbed by the wind brushing the dead leaves and Éliane's heartbeat, which was so fast and hard it echoed inside her head like a drum. Alive! She was alive. Shizelle hadn't become a murderer following irrational orders.

"I'm so sorry," Shizelle said at last, sobbing. Éliane hadn't seen her crying in years. "She said she would send me underground until everyone forgot about me and stopped bringing me food if I didn't obey."

Still frozen by shock, Éliane gritted her teeth. How could the High Seer threaten one of her own guards with starvation to commit murder? It was against every teaching of Aurië. Shadows had invaded her heart, leading her to behave like a disciple of Nunia, if not like the evil goddess herself. Éliane never imagined the High Seer could go this far. It was unprecedented.

Finally finding the strength to move and get up, Éliane offered her hand to Shizelle, who still lay on the ground, her tear-filled eyes staring at the canopy.

Once they were both back on their feet, Éliane looked Shizelle in the eye and said, "We won't let her dictate our future anymore."

Shizelle nodded and hugged Éliane closely, asking for her forgiveness again and again until Éliane ordered her to stop.

"We should go together to Fahein and tell everything to She-Who-Sees-All," Shizelle said. "She'll do something, won't she?"

Éliane blinked. "Were there any witnesses when the High Seer asked you to kill me?"

Unsurprisingly, Shizelle shook her head. "I have the night-shell. Doesn't it prove that I was sent to kill you? She wouldn't have given me one otherwise."

"She'll say you stole it," Éliane said. "It'll be her word against ours. She-Who-Sees-All will never side with us. Despite her name, she can't see the past more than regular seers."

"Then what? Should we just run away together?"

Éliane took a moment to think. It sounded like the most natural option, but it was too risky. "If you don't come back," she said, "the High Seer will send people after us. Go back to the temple and tell her you did what she asked."

Shizelle winced. "She asked me to bring back proof."

"Proof?"

"Your eyes."

Éliane tensed, imagining Shizelle removing her eyes out of her skull with her dagger. If pain wasn't involved, she would have gladly given them to Shizelle to spare her the High Seer's fury. But it wasn't only the pain. Her eyes were her connection to Aurië and what granted Éliane her seer abilities. Losing them was like losing a piece of her soul.

"I'll find a solution," Shizelle said very fast. "I'll kill a boar and show its head to Aurië, then take its eyes out when they're yellow enough. I might even find someone in Howe willing to tamper with them, so they look like a seer's."

Éliane bit her lip, thinking. Could a dead animal's eyes change like those of a nun undergoing the sightening ritual? She wasn't even sure it would work for a living one, but nobody had ever tried making a seer out of a beast. The mere thought of it sounded ridiculous.

"I'll make it work," Shizelle said, not oblivious to Éliane's skeptical look. "Don't worry about me."

"You can't ask me not to worry about you."

"Then worry all you want, but don't stop me. I'll find a way to convince the High Seer of your death, so she doesn't look for you anymore."

Éliane felt a lump growing in her throat. Shizelle almost killed her a few minutes ago, driven by fear and despair, and now she was risking her own life to protect her. Because if the High Seer uncovered Shizelle's deception, she wouldn't hesitate to order her execution for treason. Treason meant a death sentence carried by Aurië himself, his light and warmth slowly but surely leading the tied convict to die of thirst or exposure.

"Leave the trail," Shizelle continued. "Find a safe place and don't come back until there's a new High Seer."

This could take decades, Éliane knew. Shizelle was asking her to give up her life and never see her friend again. Did she have a choice? If she wanted to stay alive, Éliane had to do as Shizelle said. Leave, hide, and build a new life. But what about her eyes? It would give her nature away immediately, and soon enough words of a wandering seer would reach the High Seer's ears.

As if hearing her thoughts, Shizelle took a box out of her pocket and showed its content to Éliane. Colored lenses. "I didn't steal the night-shell, but I stole this. I…"—she paused, visibly searching her words—"I anticipated *failing* the mission the High Seer gave me, and thought you might need this to hide."

Colored lenses helped seers keep their nature hidden, so they wouldn't encounter prejudice—or worse—when traveling to places less welcoming of their kind. The pair Shizelle took from the temple's supplies were brown and would perfectly conceal her yellow pupils. It was the most common color available at the temple. The disappearance of one pair would likely go unnoticed.

She placed the box in her backpack before saying, "Let's go hunt this boar."

"No," Shizelle said. "I'll take care of it myself. You need to go."

"I won't leave until I know you have what you need to remain safe at the temple," Éliane said firmly, but not unkindly. "Consider it my parting gift to you, my friend."

Exhaling loudly, Shizelle nodded. Then she hugged Éliane one more time and whispered in her ear, "My sister."

Chapter Six

ÉLIANE

Leaving the trail meant leaving its safety, but Éliane had no choice. Now that Shizelle was gone, she was on her own and had to leave behind the things that betrayed her connection to Aurië. It meant the pilgrimage route, her yellow eyes, and her pilgrim attire. Keeping only regular clothes on her, she folded the robe and placed it in the hole Shizelle had dug for her before going back to the temple, then covered it with dirt and leaves. Her robe hidden, she washed her hands with the water from her flask and opened the box Shizelle stole. It included not only the lenses but also a small mirror, thin gloves and a flask of sun-water to rinse and manipulate the lenses safely. She had never used lenses before, but knew from other seers that they were uncomfortable to wear.

It took her multiple attempts to get the lenses to fit correctly. They made her want to rub her eyes, and she fought that urge constantly during the next hours she spent traveling east into the woods. The sun was already low in the sky, and soon the trees engulfed Éliane in darkness. She wouldn't sleep in a warm bed tonight. Instead, she found a clearing and set up her tent near a fire she struggled to start. She sat in front of the dancing flames for a long time, aware of every noise around her. The hooting owls, the howling wolves, the squeaking rodents, the whispering wind. She was in dangerous territory, and only the fire protected her against the curious beasts that might want to steal the food in her backpack or turn Éliane into their meal.

She added more branches to the fire before going into her tent. Despite exhaustion, she couldn't sleep more than fifteen minutes in a row. She kept waking up, worried that her fire had gone out, or that a bear was sneaking into the tent. Twice she almost threw a sun-shell toward a shadow, before realizing it was only a rabbit going back to its den or a fox looking for prey.

Aurië rose early, telling Éliane it was time to move on. Still tired but having no choice but to keep going, Éliane gathered her belongings and put the fire out before continuing her journey. She didn't know where she was going. Her map focused on the pilgrimage trail, so the best she could do was try to get away from it as much as she could. She knew the names of the more distant villages, but didn't know which one she would reach once out of the forest. Orienting herself was a nightmare, and several times she wondered if she had already passed a tree or a clearing.

Two more nights passed. Each time, she struggled to sleep, worrying about nocturnal creatures or about Shizelle. Was she still alive? Did she successfully trick the High Seer into believing she had killed Éliane? Not knowing was torture. A torture that might not end for a long time.

On the fourth day, she finally reached a new landmark. A rivulet. She hadn't been walking in circles. She still didn't know where she was going, and worried that going down the rivulet would bring her too close to her starting point. So instead, she went upstream, praying Aurië to bring her to a safe place.

Her wish was granted when finally, after an hours-long hike, she reached a trail following the water, and at the end of the trail, she found a clearing. At its center stood a house—or rather a mansion, considering its size—with two stories, steep roof pitches, and too many arched windows to count them. What impressed Éliane more than the mansion itself was the snow covering the tiles and most of the dark brown bricks. White powder covered the clearing, as if the clouds above the mansion had poured snow above the house but spared the rest of the forest. Despite the eerie climatic phenomenon, the house itself and its smoking chimney looked peaceful, almost welcoming. Perhaps the people living there would let Éliane stay for the night and give her much-needed directions.

As she approached the house, the door opened, and a woman emerged from inside. She was tall like a young tree. Next to her, Shizelle would have looked like a child. She was so tall that Éliane wondered if she was one of those ogres from legend and if she should flee before ending up in her belly. Her skin was as pale as the surrounding snow and her face as beautiful as the moon. Two braids as dark as the night fell on each of her shoulders, creating a sharp contrast with the whiteness of the dress she wore. She was the stunning opposite of Éliane who had curly light brown hair, bronze skin, and a short stature.

"Are you lost, child?" the giant asked, a soft smile on her face.

"I'm afraid I am."

"Please come in, then. Dulcetta just made some tea."

Éliane hesitated. The giant's eagerness to help her felt almost too good to be true. What if she was an ogre, after all?

"I won't eat you," she said, as if reading Éliane's mind. "I know I'm tall like one, but I'm not an ogre."

Flushing with unease—did she offend her?—Éliane followed the giant inside the house. Her senses got immediately assaulted by the delicious smells of baked apples and cinnamon. Six regularly sized women sat at a round table in what looked like the living room. Each had a slice of apple pie and a teacup in front of her.

As soon as she saw Éliane, one woman stood up and said, "I didn't know we were having a guest today. I'll fetch one more cup." She was a short, pudgy woman with a round, dimple-pecked face, blond hair, and green eyes rarely seen in the region.

"You're very kind, Dulce," the giant said. Then she turned to the others and said, "Ladies, please meet"—she paused, likely realizing that she didn't know Éliane's name—"your new sister."

Éliane frowned uncontrollably. Their new *sister*? What trap did she get herself into?

"So she's not only passing?" one of the women asked.

"This is up to her, of course," the giant said, looking at Éliane with a warm smile on her face. "But something tells me she's not merely lost in the woods and will need my hospitality. At least for a while. Like yourselves, ladies."

The five women—now six, since Dulcetta had just come back with a teacup and a plate for Éliane—nodded and started introducing themselves.

"My name is Aralie."

"And I'm Brune."

"Carmélia."

"Dulcetta."

"Esmée."

"Flavie."

"And I'm Lady of Clairemont, but you can simply call me Lady," the giant said, inviting Éliane to join them at the table.

Éliane did as she was told and sat between Lady and Dulcetta, who poured tea inside her cup. These women didn't look like they were part of the same family. From their skin tones to their facial features, they all came from a different corner of the world. Yet they considered each other sisters. How did Lady fit in the picture? Éliane hadn't planned to stay here more than a night or two, the time to figure out her next steps, but her curiosity was piqued. Perhaps Lady was right. Perhaps Éliane would stay here for a while.

Dulcetta asked, "How shall we call you?"

Éliane considered using a false name, but her given name was so common in the region that it felt unnecessary. With the lenses concealing her yellow pupils, she was just an average young woman with an average name and average looks. Nothing to make her stand out. After drinking a mouthful of tea, she answered. "I'm Éliane."

"Well," Lady said, "welcome to Sanctuary, Éliane."

Chapter Seven

ÉLIANE

Sanctuary wasn't only Lady of Clairemont's house, Éliane quickly found out. It was, as its name implied, a refuge for unfortunate women who needed a home when their previous one had become unsafe, and a shrine to Ido, the Earth-God. Each woman staying in Sanctuary served the deity when Lady required it, hence why they called themselves a sisterhood. Sisters in hardship and sisters in service.

"Want to help us carve some gems tomorrow?" Dulcetta asked Éliane after walking her to her bedroom. In the dimly lit room stood a wrought-iron bed frame surrounded by candelabras adorning the walls. A small window overlooked the snowy clearing and beyond, the woods in which Éliane had lost herself.

She closed the crimson velvet curtains, plunging the room into darkness. "Is that something you often do here?"

"Yes," Dulcetta said, lighting a candle. "There's a mine in the inner sanctum under Sanctuary in which Lady collects gems and stones.

We carve them so she can trade them against food with Julien, the merchant who visits us every month."

Sanctuary must have been built here as a shrine to Ido because of the mine, Éliane thought. Worshipping the Earth-God on a place where his gifts were abundant made sense, the same way Aurië's temple was in the driest, sunniest place in the country.

Chasing away the memories of her former life, Éliane said, "I'd love to help, but I've never carved before."

"You'll learn. Aralie can teach you. She's been living in Sanctuary for six years now and has become quite the gem-carver."

Éliane wanted to ask Dulcetta why Aralie had needed a refuge for all this time, what she fled, but fatigue was overtaking her body. Tomorrow, she told herself. Tomorrow, she would learn more about gem carving, Sanctuary, the six women calling themselves sisters, and Lady of Clairemont.

***

"What did you do before coming to Sanctuary?" Aralie asked Éliane after showing her how to use the grinding wheel.

Éliane should have prepared her story, but the past days had been so focused on surviving in the woods and worrying about Shizelle's fate that she had completely forgotten about it.

Thankfully, after an uncomfortable silence, Dulcetta said, "It's okay if you don't want to tell us now. You'll tell us when you're ready. If that makes you more comfortable, I'm sure some of us won't mind sharing first."

Aralie cleared her throat and said, "Dulce probably told you already how long I've been here. Five years and ten months. Almost six years."

Éliane nodded quietly, waiting for Aralie to continue. To her surprise, Dulcetta spoke instead. "Aralie's husband is a violent man, but his family is even worse. They never accepted that Aralie left the marriage they arranged."

"These vultures swore to look for me until their last breath to make me pay," Aralie said bitterly, as she pushed a stone against the grinding wheel, smoothing it. "So far they haven't found me." As she pronounced the words, a shade formed above Aralie's head. Guilt, Éliane recognized. What did she do to leave her in-law's clutches, she wondered?

"Ido protects us," Carmélia, who was assembling a necklace, said after looking reverently to the ground in that gesture Éliane had seen the Earth-God disciples do when they visited Aurië's temple.

"Ido and Lady," Dulcetta added.

Smiling nervously, Éliane asked in a whisper, "Can you tell me more about Lady?" She didn't fear the woman, but didn't trust her yet. Lady had offered Éliane bed and board without asking much in return, which was typical of disciples of Ido, but her imposing figure still loomed within Éliane's mind. Something told her she wasn't simply a tall woman. She was something *more*, and that *more* was yet to be determined. It could be insignificant or deadly. Ogres weren't the only creatures threatening humans in legends. Éliane knew it was a silly thought, especially after the High Seer, a very human person, plotted her murder, but she couldn't help but wonder what Lady's nature was. Could she be a godkin of Ido? The Earth-God was often depicted as a tall man in his corporeal form. This could explain Lady's unusual stature.

Éliane's theory quickly fell apart when Dulcetta said, "She hasn't shared much about her life before Sanctuary, besides being the daughter of a usurped queen from a faraway country."

"She was a *princess*," Carmélia said, as if the word tasted like honey.

"That was before the usurper murdered the queen and chased the surviving members of the royal family away."

"Which is, according to what she told Aralie, only her."

"She never told me that," Aralie argued. "I *deducted* it, but I can't be certain."

Dulcetta nodded and said, turning to Éliane, "Lady is very sensitive about her past. She prefers to focus on the present. Serving Ido and caring for the sisters is what brings her joy. Not rehashing what happened to her family."

"Do you know what country she comes from?" Éliane asked cautiously. Perhaps Lady came from a place where humans were taller than average.

To her disappointment, all the sisters sitting around her—the six of them, as they were all participating in gem crafting—shook their head.

"Your guess is as good as mine," Dulcetta said.

"The only country I know of who had a brutal change in leadership is Streya, but it was two centuries ago," Carmélia offered.

"She would be very old if she comes from this place. It's impossible."

"Unless she's a godkin?" Éliane blurted, immediately cursing herself silently for being unable to keep her theory to herself. She had arrived not even a day ago, and she was already questioning her host's nature in front of six women who owed her their survival. Not the wisest action. Again, that blasted curiosity of hers!

Dulcetta's eyes opened wide. "She's the daughter of a queen, not of Ido," she argued, as if a god would stop himself from lying with a queen to spare a prince consort's feelings. Before Éliane could answer, she added, "We would know it if she was a godkin. She'd have some supernatural powers, wouldn't she?"

Éliane nodded reluctantly, thinking about Dame Héloïse and her light. The sisters would have surely noticed if Lady had inherited divine abilities. She had to stop asking pointed questions. Whoever Lady was, she wouldn't find out by harassing the poor women who had warmly welcomed her as one of them.

"The world is a large place," Aralie said eventually, her tone final, as if she didn't like Lady's past being questioned. "We don't know all the countries it's made of and all the people inhabiting them. Maybe she comes from beyond the ocean."

Everyone nodded, Éliane included. The conversation was over.

As she followed Aralie's instructions, Éliane couldn't help but glance at the shades appearing and disappearing around her. Guilt, regret, sadness, fear—they all flashed above Aralie's head, separately or together, sometimes blending in a cloud of sorrow only Éliane could see. It wasn't only her shades that betrayed her emotions. Her pale face, too, was marked by her past. Éliane didn't know how old Aralie was, but the wrinkles on her forefront and cheeks made her look older than she probably was.

"She misses her son," Dulcetta later told Éliane, as they set up the table for lunch while the other sisters were busy cleaning and cooking. "She hasn't seen him since leaving her husband."

"Six years ago?"

"Oh no, more than that. Aralie spent two years on the run before she found Sanctuary. Her son was just a kid when she left. He must be a young man by now. She tried fleeing with him, but her in-laws prevented her from doing so."

That explained the shades. Guilt and regret at having left her son behind to save herself. Sadness and fear, wondering how he was doing, if he was still alive and well, the same way Éliane worried about Shizelle. Aralie was probably living in a near-constant agony. It had been only a few days since Éliane had been separated from Shizelle. She couldn't imagine living for almost a decade without knowing her fate.

The food and table ready, Éliane, Dulcetta, and the other sisters sat, ready to eat, but Lady was nowhere to be seen. Did she absent herself? No, she had to be here. Éliane and Dulcetta had set up the table for eight people.

"Lady will join us momentarily," Dulcetta said, as if hearing Éliane's thoughts. "She must be busy outside."

Outside, where the snow fell above the house while sparing the rest of the forest. Was it a blessing from Ido, Éliane wondered? But the elements weren't his domain, not truly. Éliane had learned Ido's story during her studies at the temple, and his tortuous love story with Cyma, the Sky-Goddess who controlled the weather. Perhaps Ido, on Lady's request, had asked Cyma to snow above the mansion, and she had granted them what was an odd wish, for nobody wanted their land to be constantly covered in snow. The phenomenon was too strange to leave Éliane unbothered. Soon she would have to ask someone about it. Aralie or Dulcetta, probably, as they seemed eager to open up compared to the other sisters.

"Someone should go look for her," Carmélia said at last. "The pies are going to be cold."

Hesitantly, Éliane said, "I can go." She hadn't left the inside of the house since arriving the day before and wanted a chance to look at the eerie snow—and at whatever she could find that could tell her more about Sanctuary and Lady.

Dulcetta nodded, pointing at the back of the house. "She's probably fetching water in the well, or doing something in her workshop."

A bit surprised at how none of the sisters offered to go instead—Éliane didn't know the mansion well yet, so she had expected someone to argue—but happy to get her wish granted, she gave Dulcetta a nod and left the dining room.

The back door creaked open under her gentle push, revealing the white clearing behind the house. She saw the well in the distance, close to the edge of the forest, but Lady was nowhere near it. The workshop it was then.

As she walked toward the shed, Éliane couldn't help but look down. The snow her shoes sank into looked absolutely normal. She hadn't had a chance to see a lot of snow in her life, since the orphanage and the temple were in the driest part of the country, but the few times she had seen and touched the white powder weren't different from what she experienced now. The clouds above her head might not be a natural phenomenon, but the snow they poured was.

What wasn't normal, though, was its sudden change of color. The white blanket had turned bright red, as if a pool of blood had soaked into it. Her pulse quickening, Éliane followed what wasn't a pool but actually a trail, leading right to the shed's entrance. A voice in her mind told her to run away, while another told her Lady was perhaps in danger, attacked by an intruder who had dragged her inside her own shed. But even if it was an intruder, Éliane couldn't do much against them. Her sun-shells were inside her room, hidden deep inside her backpack so nobody could find them and guess where she came from. She had to run back to the house and get some help. But what if it was a trap, she wondered? What if the sisters had sent her to the shed so Lady could murder her for some sinister reason? What if she was an ogre, after all? Éliane had to run into the woods. But she had nothing on her! She wouldn't survive one day in the wilderness without her belongings.

The conflicting thoughts kept fighting in her mind while her legs kept moving toward the shed, as if a supernatural force was possessing her. What devilry had overtaken her body, leading her right into a trap? An irresistible curiosity her anxiety couldn't tame? She didn't know, and when she regained control of herself, it was too late. She had already pushed the door open.

An apron tied around her waist, Lady turned her tall body all at once to face Éliane, who didn't know if it was the blood on the woman's clothes or the butcher knife in her hand that made her scream.

Chapter Eight

ÉLIANE

Éliane's scream eventually faded, leaving room for silent, frozen terror. The acrid smell of blood overwhelmed her senses the same way apples and cinnamon had done so the day before, except this time, it made her gag.

"Don't be scared, child," Lady said, her face stern, not easing Éliane's fears one bit. But to Éliane's surprise, she put the knife down and stepped to the side, revealing the chopped body of a boar. "The last food supplies we purchased were for seven people, and the merchant won't be back for another two weeks. I had no choice but to hunt a boar so we could feed everyone well, especially since we have a feast tomorrow." She looked around her, gesturing at the floor. "I clearly made a bloody mess of the place. My apologies if this caused you any distress."

A blend of confusion and shame filled Éliane. Did she just take Lady for a murderous ogre when she was simply preparing meat for the sisters? For her, since she was the new mouth to feed?

"Well, I, I," she stuttered, unable to find the right words. She took a deep breath in to calm herself, then managed to articulate, "Lunch is ready."

Her stomach turning sick at the view and smell of the dead boar, Éliane promptly stepped back and closed the door. If she had salivated at the pies a few minutes ago, her appetite was now gone. The High Seer's jealousy and betrayal, Shizelle's unknown fate, her discomfort at the eerie snowing, her unfounded fears about Lady's nature, the sight of blood and guts, everything blended into a pool of distress inside her mind, and tears rolled down her cheeks uncontrollably. She wanted to apologize to Lady for screaming needlessly, to the sisters for suspecting them to send her into a trap, to Shizelle for not going back to the temple with her and confront the High Seer together—no matter how low their chances of winning were—and to herself for not being braver.

Collecting herself with difficulty, Éliane walked back toward the manor, careful not to step into the blood-soaked snow. Inside, she found the sisters at the table the same way she had left them, except for a concerned look on Dulcetta's face.

"Are you all right, Éliane?" she asked her, unsurprisingly. Éliane had no doubt she looked terrible after the screaming and the crying that had happened outside.

"I'm fine," she said. "Lady was preparing a boar in her workshop."

She hoped it was enough of an explanation to justify her discomfort, and that the sisters wouldn't judge her weak or oversensitive for being disturbed by the view of a dead animal—though it wasn't the real reason she had been shaken. Thankfully, it was enough, because Dulcetta nodded and nobody commented.

Soon Lady joined them at the table, her bloody apron gone and her arms and hands clean as if she hadn't been butchering a beast a few minutes before. Éliane almost wondered if she had dreamed the scene.

"Let's thank Ido for sharing his earthly body with us to grow the food we are about to eat," Lady said before Carmélia cut the pies.

As Éliane chewed unenthusiastically, a thought hit her mind. All the food she had eaten in Sanctuary so far—only a couple of meals, but still—had been devoid of meat, and for a good reason. Disciples of Ido ate exclusively cereals and vegetables. Killing and eating an animal was an affront to the Earth-God, who encouraged his disciples to abstain from it. Each time disciples of Ido had visited Aurië's temple, Éliane and the other nuns had cooked meatless dishes for their guests. So why had Lady hunted a boar? Wasn't it against her principles?

"Pardon my curiosity," Éliane said at last, "but I was under the impression that Ido condemned the consumption of meat. Are we really going to eat the boar?"

Aralie coughed, as if pie had gone the wrong way. The other sisters remained silent. They visibly didn't expect Éliane to ask that question.

After a brief but uncomfortable silence, Lady steepled her fingers in front of her face and said, her voice flat but with a hint of reproach, "It is indeed forbidden for people like me to consume an animal's flesh. But this restriction only applies to me. Ido doesn't expect you and the other sisters to abide by the same rules, especially in dire times. If you still prefer to abstain from meat, then so be it."

Éliane felt the urge to justify herself, to say that she didn't mind eating meat or vegetables or whatever the sisters cooked for her, but she kept quiet. In a couple of sentences, Lady had managed to make her feel guilty for what sounded like insolence. Who questioned their host's ways in their own home? Éliane had learned better manners, but her anxious curiosity made her forget her own principles.

"I'll happily eat the meat if this allows you to respect the Earth-God's wishes," Éliane whispered, wishing she had said nothing.

Lady nodded and resumed eating her own slice of pie. Then, when Éliane thought the matter was settled, Lady placed her fork on the edge of her plate and said matter-of-factly, "You know a lot about our ways, child." Éliane didn't respond, waiting for the woman to continue. "You haven't told us where you lived before and what you fled in the woods."

Éliane glanced at Dulcetta, hoping she would save her again by telling Lady to give Éliane time to open up, but the sister remained silent, her eyes focused on her own plate. Was she scared of Lady? No matter why Dulcetta refused to come to her aid, Éliane was alone and had to answer now if she didn't want to be ruder than she already was. What if Lady deemed her untrustworthy and kicked her out of Sanctuary? Éliane still didn't know where to go. Sanctuary was an unexpected haven, and she hoped to stay here a bit longer.

That disciples of Ido abstained from consuming meat wasn't a secret. A lot of people knew it, not only disciples of other gods and goddesses. Right? Éliane learned about it at the orphanage—at least she thought so? What if it wasn't common knowledge, after all? Perhaps she learned about it just after arriving at the temple. It had been only a few years, but it felt like a lifetime ago and she couldn't remember. All she knew was that she couldn't tell Lady and the sisters that she was a seer. Not until she could trust them.

Eventually, she settled for a half-truth. "My former guardian is the daughter of a disciple of Cyma, so she taught me a thing or two about the gods and their ways. That was before she tried to kill me."

The High Seer was indeed the daughter of a disciple of the Sky-Goddess, and it was technically true that she had been Éliane's guardian for a couple of years, between her departure from the orphanage and her seventeenth birthday, but she had never acted like one. She was a teacher, an authority figure, but didn't behave motherly toward Éliane or Shizelle or any of the other orphans who joined her temple. The only difference between Mrs. Breval and the High Seer was that the latter didn't throw them out once they reached adulthood.

"Why did she try to kill you?" Lady asked, to Éliane's stupefaction. Her tone didn't convey concern or outrage, but cold inquisitiveness, as if Éliane could be guilty of her own attempted murder.

Stifling a sigh, Éliane said, "I didn't want to marry the person she picked for me. She never liked me very much, so I guess it was the tipping point for her. She got upset and attacked me. I escaped thanks to sheer luck only."

Lady stared at her for a moment, visibly thinking. Was she buying the lie? Éliane could have thought of something better, more convincing, but it was all that had come to her mind. Hopefully, Lady wouldn't press her further. Éliane had always lacked imagination, and now wasn't the time to test its poor limits.

"Is she looking for you?" Lady asked at last, filling Éliane with relief.

"I don't know," she said truthfully. "Maybe. All I know is that I can't go back."

"None of us can go back," Dulcetta said softly, finally speaking.

Lady nodded, her face relaxing a little. Then she said, her voice flat, "As long as you follow the rules of the house, you are welcome to stay in Sanctuary for as long as you'd like, child."

The statement sounded half like a promise, half like a warning. Éliane was allowed to stay, but she had to keep a low profile and stop questioning her hostess's ways. She remained silent for the rest of the meal, listening to the sisters' conversation. The two sisters sitting next to her, Carmélia and Flavie, told Éliane about their own past, as to ease her visible discomfort. Flavie was the most recent addition to Sanctuary before Éliane, and had been here for only three months. She was also the youngest, barely seventeen, and had fled an abusive uncle and her even more abusive aunt.

"We share a similar story," Flavie said gently, "though I hope your guardian didn't treat you as badly as my aunt and uncle." To illustrate her statement, she rolled up her sleeve and showed Éliane the scars on her arm, where they had hurt her in unimaginable ways. "I have more on my back, but you don't want to see it."

Éliane's heart clenched as she kept listening to Flavie's story. In comparison, she had been the luckiest girl in the world. Growing up in an orphanage wasn't the best beginning one could experience in life, but at least Mrs. Breval didn't hit the children under her care, even if she didn't feed them well or cared little about their future.

Carmélia's story was a sad tale too, though she seemed to have recovered from it. She had been in Sanctuary for a little over three years now, having arrived shortly after Brune, who had herself arrived after Aralie. She was in her early thirties now and didn't *flee* anyone. No, instead, she had fled homelessness after her husband had repudiated her for failing to give him children and her family had refused to take her back. With few prospects as a divorced woman, Sanctuary was the best thing that had happened to her.

"I have a sister in Valenmont," she said, talking about a distant city beyond the northern border. "One day, I'll leave Sanctuary and join her there. Lady taught me a lot of useful skills. I'm sure I could make a new life for myself there. When I'm ready."

Eventually, all the sisters told their own story to Éliane as they cleaned up the table. Brune was a refugee who had nowhere to go after war destroyed her home and killed her loved ones. Peace had come back to her homeland, and she often thought about going back, but she enjoyed her life in Sanctuary, away from painful memories. Dulcetta's story was similar to Aralie's, except it wasn't her in-laws she feared, but her violent husband who had sworn to find and bring her back to their home. At least, she had left before having children. As for Esmée, the shiest of the sisters who had arrived shortly before Flavie, she had been blessed with a loving husband but cursed by misfortune. Disease took him soon in their marriage and a natural disaster destroyed her house not long after. The nail in the coffin had been the appearance of debt collectors, pretending her husband had owed them more money than she could ever earn in her life. When they threatened to bring her to the neighboring country of Peridar, where slavery was still legal, to sell her so they could recoup their loss, she fled and found a new home in Sanctuary.

"None of us knew where we were going when we found Sanctuary," Dulcetta told Éliane. "It's as if the place is guiding lost souls toward it."

Éliane nodded. She had also found the place without searching for it. She didn't even know Sanctuary existed before reaching it. It was surely Lady's design, Éliane thought. For the place to remain a safe refuge, it couldn't be known by outsiders, otherwise the vengeful husbands and in-laws and debt collectors would show up at its doors all the time.

Unsurprisingly, but still to Éliane's disappointment, Lady didn't say a word about her own past. She understood the woman not wanting to talk about the circumstances that brought her here, but she would have liked to know if Sanctuary already existed before Lady arrived, or if she built the place herself. The architecture of the house betrayed the length of its existence, too long for a mere mortal's lifespan, meaning it had been standing here long before Lady.

Unless she was as old as the house, because she wasn't a mere mortal, something the sisters had vehemently denied.

"Once I'm done with the boar," Lady told the sisters, rolling up her sleeves, "I'll spend some time in the inner sanctum. You know what that means."

Éliane didn't know what that meant, but Dulcetta explained right away.

"The inner sanctum is the most sacred place in Sanctuary. It's the space underneath the house, where Lady collects gems. Only *she* can go down there."

"You've never seen what it looks like?"

Dulcetta shook her head. "Lady says it would anger Ido if someone who's not a disciple walks in the inner sanctum."

"Aren't you all disciples?" Éliane asked hesitantly. "Don't you perform rituals in his name?"

"We do, but we are only sisters, not actual disciples. Lady learned his ways in a temple. She went through the whole thing to become a true earth-worshipper. We did not, which is why we can eat the boar meat if we want to, and can't enter the inner sanctum."

Éliane cocked her head. Some parts of Aurië's temple were reserved for seers and nobody else could access them. Visitors, nuns in training, even Aurië's godkins—none of them could walk on the most sacred floor of the temple if they hadn't undergone the sightening ritual. This was surely the same with Sanctuary's inner sanctum.

"I assume the entrance is hidden or locked, so we can't get in by accident," Éliane said, worried about going through the wrong door and angering her hostess and her god. "I'd like to avoid trespassing."

Dulcetta shook her head. "The door is neither hidden nor locked, but don't worry. You won't get in by accident. If you know how to read, you'll know when you find it. You know how to read, do you?"

Éliane nodded. "Lady trusts us not to go down against her will?"

"She trusts us because we trust her word, and we respect Ido. I wouldn't want to anger a god, would you?"

"Of course I wouldn't," Éliane said very fast, shaking her head.

"Anyway, it's really dark down there. I've never been, but when I see Lady getting in and out, there's no light. She says the Earth-God prefers it this way, and her training at Ido's temple allows her to see in the darkness."

Éliane frowned. Ido's disciples, able to see in the dark? She had never heard of it. But there were a lot of other things she hadn't heard of, including things about the god she served. Had she completed her pilgrimage, she would have come back with new abilities. Which ones? That, she would only know after passing She-Who-Sees-All's test of faith and receiving her benediction. Perhaps Ido's disciples had a similar journey with uncommon rewards, like Lady's.

With the gem-carving activities completed for the day, Éliane retreated to her room. As she approached the window to look outside, she realized it was the first time in her life that she didn't share a bedroom with someone else. The orphanage had dormitories, and only the seers who completed their pilgrimage had their own private room, while nuns and young seers shared a bedroom with at least another person.

Snow was falling again on the house, covering the clearing in whiteness while the surrounding woods remained indubitably green with hints of orange, announcing autumn. Soon the solstice would be there, and shortly after, the first natural snowflakes that would cover the landscape. Sanctuary wouldn't be an anomaly anymore. Éliane still hadn't asked Dulcetta or any of the other sisters about the strange phenomenon, but after what happened this morning, she preferred not to ask questions for a while. Instead, she kept watching outside, wondering how Shizelle fared, if the High Seer was proud of herself, and how long she would stay here, in Sanctuary. Perhaps she could travel to Valenmont with Carmélia, if she managed to strike enough of a friendship with the sister.

Evening came, and with it, another meal shared with the sisters and Lady. Flavie had cooked the meal tonight—boar ragout, and frumenty for those who preferred to abstain from eating meat. Éliane wondered when her turn to cook would come. No matter when it happened, she was ready for it. She had worked in the temple's kitchen to prepare meals for dozens of people. Cooking for eight was a formality.

As she filled her spoon with ragout, she realized there were only seven of them at the table. Before she could consider asking, Dulcetta said, "Where is Aralie?"

"I saw her crocheting in the living room after lunch," Carmélia said. "I'm sure she'll be there in a mi—"

"She's gone." Lady spoke with a stern voice, as if the words she had just pronounced hurt her.

"Gone?" Dulcetta said, her eyes opening wide.

"She asked me not to tell any of you, but she had been thinking about going back home to find her son for a while," Lady continued. "More than thinking," she said before Dulcetta could speak, "actually *planning*. Today's conversation about your respective pasts was the catalyst that convinced her to leave. She made her decision in the afternoon. I tried to convince her to stay a bit longer, but she had set her mind. I'm sorry I didn't tell you, but I had no idea she would leave today, and like I said, I was sworn to secrecy. She didn't want to worry any of you."

None of the sisters answered. By the look on Dulcetta's face, Éliane knew she didn't trust a single word Lady had pronounced.

Chapter Nine

ÉLIANE

"She would have never left without saying goodbye," Carmélia whispered, under Dulcetta's approving look.

"She would have never left, period," Dulcetta added.

The two sisters discussed privately in the kitchen with Éliane while cleaning the dishes. Éliane wished she could have nodded approvingly, but she had been at Sanctuary for less than two days. She barely knew Aralie. Her opinion was limited to a handful of interactions with the woman and what others told her. And she saw the shades hovering above Aralie, betraying her guilt and regrets. What if Lady was telling the truth? But she didn't say a word. Éliane didn't want to upset the two sisters, and they may be right, after all.

If Aralie hadn't left, then where was she, Éliane wondered?

"I checked her room," Dulcetta said. "Some of her things are gone."

"It still doesn't make sense. She never ever told me or you or Brune than she considered going back. Sure, she missed her son... but she'd been here for so long." Carmélia paused, shaking her head as to clear her thoughts. "I don't know."

"I don't know either," Dulcetta confided. "I don't think any of us know."

"I wish Lady would have told us," Carmélia whispered. "We could have helped her convince Aralie to stay."

"Maybe that's why she didn't want you to know," Éliane offered, hoping her suggestion wouldn't make the sisters defensive. "She probably knew that it would have been too hard to leave with all of you asking her to stay."

Carmélia cocked her head, visibly considering her argument. Then she said, sighing, "Maybe. I still struggle to believe that she's gone. You didn't know her like we did..."

Éliane didn't argue, because Carmélia was right—and, Éliane realized, because she struggled to accept Aralie's departure too. The woman had been so kind to her, teaching her how to carve gems just a few hours ago, and now she was gone. Was it, somehow, Éliane's fault? Did she shatter a delicate balance with her arrival and her improper questions? She was certain a guilt-shaped shade was now circling above her own head, and was grateful nobody could see it.

"Ladies," a voice said from the corridor. Lady leaned to walk under the door frame, too low for her stature, and said, "Sorry to interrupt your conversation, but it's getting late. You remember what day tomorrow is, don't you?"

Dulcetta and Carmélia glanced at each other apprehensively before Dulcetta said, raising a finger in the air, "The equinox!"

"I'm glad you haven't forgotten," Lady said. "This will be a busy day for me, and I'll need your help." She looked at Éliane. "With Aralie gone, I'll welcome your help too, child."

Éliane nodded, unsure of what was expected of her. The equinoxes were synonymous of rituals for many deities, Aurië included, but she didn't know what Ido wanted. She would find out in the morning.

***

Éliane didn't sleep well. She tossed and turned, her mind dwelling on Aralie's departure in between anxious moments spent thinking about Shizelle. On her mind was also the upcoming ritual, and Lady's expectations. Ido's expectations. Aurië's expectations, too. Éliane had devoted herself to the Sun-God, and if Aurië wasn't a jealous deity who forbade the worship of others, he still expected his disciples to honor him *first*. Éliane may have left the temple to save her life, but it didn't change who she was. No matter the lenses hiding her yellow pupils, she was a seer. Tomorrow, she would have to fulfill the promise she had made five years ago *and* please the god whose disciples offered her a safe refuge.

Dulcetta woke her up early in the morning from the half-sleep state she had spent the night in. She followed her guidance absent-mindedly, too tired to answer by anything more than a nod.

"Lady is already outside preparing the ritual with Brune and Carmélia," Dulcetta told her. "Esmée and Flavie are busy with cooking duties—the equinox means a feast—and I'm supposed to carve some gems now that Aralie is gone. So you'll take my role in the ritual, understood?"

Éliane blinked and nodded, yawning instead of asking what her role was. Thankfully, Dulcetta wasn't blind to her predicament because she said, "It won't be hard. Just do exactly what Brune and Carmélia do, and you'll be fine. Also, come drink a cup of tea before heading outside. You look like you haven't slept in ages."

Dulcetta prepared black tea flavored with bergamot, which accompanied Esmée's financiers to perfection. The hot drink and cakes filled Éliane's stomach and helped her fully wake up, so she could join Lady and the two sisters outside.

"You arrive just in time," Lady said. "We're ready to begin."

The woman sat in the middle of offerings. Baskets of fruits, vegetables, wheat, mushrooms, bread, and jars filled with milk and wine encircled her, representing the different foods and beverages created thanks to Ido's body. A bramble crown adorned Lady's head, giving a gloomy touch to her attire—a brown and orange tunic reminding Éliane of the clothes she used to wear at the temple, except for their darker colors.

Brune and Carmélia stood next to Lady, outside of the circle of offerings. The sisters were so short and Lady so tall that even seated, the top of her skull was higher than their heads. To Éliane's relief, Carmélia discreetly signaled her to come closer. She placed herself to her left and followed her movements. Only Lady spoke, reciting a long prayer to the Earth-God in a language Éliane didn't recognize. It was, perhaps, the tongue people spoke in her homeland. Meanwhile, Brune and Carmélia moved the offerings in a curious dance Éliane did her best to follow, wondering how long the ritual would last. What she knew was that she had never seen such an odd ritual before.

Eventually, Lady fell silent. She closed her eyes and remained still like a statue. The sisters lifted a vase filled with wine and poured it over her head, soaking the bramble crown and the woman's hair. Some wine ran down her back and reached the snow, forming a crimson pool that reminded Éliane of the bloody trail she had followed the day before. She resisted the urge to gag as she remembered the smell inside the workshop.

It's just wine, she told herself. *It's wine and it was only a boar.*

Brune showed a cup to Éliane, telling her without words to take it and fill it with milk for Lady. Ignoring her growing discomfort, she did as she was instructed and brought the cup to the giant's mouth, who drank mouthful after mouthful of the white liquid.

"Let's finish the ritual," Lady said.

Brune and Carmélia positioned themselves on each side of Lady and took her hand. Then, they invited Éliane to hold their other hand, forming a circle. Éliane was glad she wasn't holding Lady's hand, because what happened next stupefied her.

The woman talked again in that foreign language of hers, but louder, and this time the earth reacted to her words. Channeling Ido's powers, the new prayer made the ground sprout with plants, emerging from the snow in a green explosion. This part didn't worry Éliane, but as the plants kept growing, the clouds above their heads dispersed, revealing the sun and, low on the horizon, a pale crescent moon. Sunbeams flooded the clearing, their reflection on the snow blinding Éliane, but she still saw through her squinted eyes a giant shade appear around Lady. It lasted only a few seconds before vanishing at the same time the clouds reconstituted themselves in the sky.

"Enough," Lady said, out of breath. She let go the sisters' hands. "We're done."

She rose and darted toward the house, ignoring the sisters and the offerings and the plants. Brune and Carmélia gathered the unused foods and drinks while Éliane stared at Lady, paralyzed with disquietude and only able to think about the shade and whisper, "What was that?"

Chapter Ten

ÉLIANE

Immediately after entering the house, Lady absented herself by going down into the inner sanctum. "The ritual exhausted me," she explained. "Ido will help me recover, especially after such a successful ritual."

Éliane didn't know what successful meant—finishing it? growing plants? clearing the clouds?—but she knew there was something wrong with the shade she saw. Not only was it massive, but it was still here. Éliane couldn't see it, but she knew it still hovered above Lady's head, because it didn't form or disappear like shades tied to a temporary emotion. The *sun* revealed it, meaning Lady was able to hide her shades almost as well as the High Seer. But Lady wasn't a seer. How could she master this difficult skill without enduring the sightening ritual? Without practicing at a temple of Aurië for years? Not only it didn't make sense, but it scared Éliane. Lady wasn't an ogre, but she still wasn't a regular human. What if she had lied to the sisters and wasn't a deposed princess? None of the six women were seers, so they couldn't know about the sun revealing Lady's shades.

There was, also, the nature of the shade itself. Éliane wished the sun hadn't blinded her, or the cloud would have reformed later, so she could have assessed the shade. She was unsure but believed she had seen either sorrow or anger. Perhaps a blend of both—grief? frustration? resentment? guilt? No matter was it was, Éliane had never seen such a large one. Whatever feelings Lady harbored, they had lived inside her mind for a long, long time, maturing and growing enormously.

It's a miracle she's still alive, Éliane thought. Most people living with such an intense emotion were either consumed by it, succumbing to a disease called Nunia's night, or ended their lives themselves. Whatever Lady was, she was strong enough to resist and keep living.

Down in the inner sanctum, Lady missed the equinox feast. This meant Éliane could ask the burning questions that filled her mind. But first, she showed respect to Esmée and Flavie by devouring the dishes they prepared. Boar roast, baked potatoes and turnips, pumpkin and mushroom soups, bread and cheese, sweet wine and apple pie—Éliane had never eaten so much food.

"I wish Aralie was here to enjoy the feast," Dulcetta said.

Éliane and the other sisters nodded silently. Today was supposed to be joyful, but Aralie's departure was still on everybody's mind.

"Too bad Lady isn't here to enjoy it either," Flavie added.

"Let's make sure to keep some leftovers for her," Carmélia offered. "She should be back up by the evening."

Time to ask questions, Éliane told herself. "Does she often need to rest in the inner sanctum?" she asked, seizing the segue offered to her.

Brune shook her head. "It happens occasionally, but not that much. I'm not sure why today's ritual tired her. It wasn't longer than past equinoxes and solstices."

"She's getting older," Carmélia said, shrugging.

Éliane cleared her throat. "Could it be the sun?" She couldn't share her vision of the giant shade, but Brune and Carmélia saw the sunlight too, and how Lady immediately stopped the ritual afterward. Regardless of what caused the weather phenomenon, Lady preferred to avoid direct sunlight.

"Lady likes the clouds above Sanctuary," Brune conceded. "I've always found it odd, since Ido and Aurië are friends, but she said once that snow reminds her of her homeland."

There was definitely more to it than mere melancholy, but Éliane didn't insist. Instead, she asked, "Do you know how she does it? The constant clouds."

"She never said," Brune said. "We all wonder."

"It must be a favor from Cyma," Dulcetta offered, to which Éliane nodded as she shared the same opinion. It still didn't explain *why* the gods agreed to Lady's request for constant clouds and snow. One more mystery her unending curiosity would feel unsatisfied not having an answer to.

After the feast, Éliane offered to help Dulcetta with gem crafting, to which the sister agreed eagerly. Aralie wasn't there to teach Éliane, but she still managed to polish the stones and assist Dulcetta with her tasks.

"How would you describe Lady's personality?" Éliane asked as matter-of-factly as she could, trying to convince Dulcetta that she was only making conversation, while in truth she couldn't resist trying to learn more about her mysterious hostess.

"You've seen her," Dulcetta answered. "I know her stature is imposing, but she's always calm and protective of us and Sanctuary."

"Always?"

"She has her difficult moments, like everyone."

"How difficult?"

"You *are* a curious bird, aren't you?" Dulcetta said. Before Éliane could justify herself, the sister gave her a broad smile and said, "Don't worry. I was like you, too, when I arrived in Sanctuary. This is quite the place, and Lady is quite the woman. To answer your question, there have been times when Lady spent entire weeks in the inner sanctum, only emerging every few days to check on us. It happened only twice since I arrived, and each time Lady suffered physically and mentally from what she described was a unique form of homesickness."

"Homesickness?"

Dulcetta nodded. "She lost everything. She's a strong woman—we all are in Sanctuary—but sometimes, her past catches up on her, and she needs time to recover from the darkness invading her mind."

Nunia's night, Éliane thought. Did Lady suffer episodes of it, but recovered instead of passing like most of the disease's victims? Without seeing more of Lady's shades, since she hid them, Éliane couldn't confirm her hypothesis. Anyway, she couldn't cure the sickness. Seer Ahma had come back from his own pilgrimage with the gift of shade-cleansing, a rare ability allowing some seers to ease people's inner turmoil and heal their souls. Even if Éliane confirmed Lady suffered from Nunia's night, she couldn't help her.

Thankfully, Lady didn't seem to suffer from another episode because she came back reinvigorated for dinner. Snow fell again outside, already covering the plants that had sprouted during the equinox ritual. Lady acted as if everything was normal, and it was, except for Aralie's absence.

"Are you sure she didn't leave a letter for us?" Dulcetta asked Lady.

Lady clasped her large hands. "If she did, she didn't give it to me. You are welcome to search her room."

Carmélia and Dulcetta nodded at each other, and spent an hour searching Aralie's room after dinner. The disappointed look on their faces told Éliane their search was fruitless.

When night fell on Sanctuary, fatigue overcame Éliane. Too much food, too many emotions, too many half-answered questions, too many lingering concerns. Was Aralie safe? Did she really leave to find her son? And what about Shizelle? Éliane didn't have the energy to worry anymore and promptly fell asleep under the warmth of the blankets.

***

It was still dark when she opened her eyes. Éliane didn't know what time it was, but the lack of light filtering through the curtains told her it was still the middle of the night. A noise had stirred her mind away from the dream it was caught in. Whispers. Steps. Someone was up in Sanctuary. Someone close to her bedroom. Flavie or Brune, since their rooms were in the same part of the house.

At first, Éliane considered ignoring the noise and getting back to sleep, but the steps became louder, as if someone was running. Intrigued, she left the comfort of her bed to check the sisters weren't in trouble. The door to Carmélia's room was closed. Putting her ear against it, Éliane had no trouble hearing the sister snore loudly. Carefully, she tiptoed to Brune's room, only to find the door open and her bed empty.

"Brune?" she whispered.

Nobody answered.

Then the stairs cracked.

Éliane moved swiftly toward the staircase, only to spot Brune's silhouette already reaching the lower floor. "Brune," she whispered again, louder.

Brune kept walking down, not paying attention to Éliane. Did she ignore her? Or perhaps didn't hear her? She could be sleepwalking. Éliane had no choice but to go down the stairs. If Brune wasn't awake, she had to help her.

When Éliane reached the first floor, Brune was already turning at the end of the corridor, rushing to the kitchen. *Why is she moving so fast?* Éliane wondered. There was a nun at the temple who often sleepwalked, and Éliane had sometimes helped her back to her room. But the girl walked slowly and was easy to catch and gently wake up. Perhaps Brune wasn't asleep.

Éliane dashed to the kitchen. Empty. Brune had already left through the other door. Quickly, Éliane kept going, and caught a glimpse of Brune turning into another corridor.

"Brune!" Éliane called. "Where are you going?"

Again, no answer. For an instant, she considered giving up the chase and going back to her room. After all, Lady didn't forbid the sisters from leaving their room at night. Maybe Brune was an early riser. Éliane still didn't know what time it was. It could be close to sunrise. But her curiosity—and the feeling that Brune might be in trouble—won over her desire to leave the woman alone.

Éliane rushed to the corridor, expecting to spot Brune at the other end once more, but all she found was an empty hallway. She moved forward, ready to run after the sister, when a door caught her attention. Glowing letters adorned it, casting a blueish light in the darkness.

The entrance to the inner sanctum, Éliane thought as she touched the letters reading "Down Lies the Heart of Sanctuary." Did Brune go inside the forbidden place? She wouldn't. Not on purpose.

"Child," a voice called, startling Éliane. Next to her was Lady, holding a candle that illuminated her face. "Are you lost?"

Chapter Eleven

ÉLIANE

I'm in trouble, was the first thought that crossed Éliane's mind, quickly followed by *How didn't I see her coming?*

"I wasn't trying to enter the inner sanctum," she said very fast, taking a step back from the door. "I was only following Brune. I worried she was sleepwalking."

"Sleepwalking?" Lady said, frowning. "If this indeed happened, it would be a first. I'm sure she's sound asleep in her room."

I saw her bed empty, she wanted to say, but Lady's stern look made her feel like a fool. What if she had followed shadows? No, the silhouette was real. She had recognized Brune's long hair and gait.

"Shall we go check her room to ease your mind?" the giant offered.

Gulping with unease, Éliane nodded. Lady would see by herself that Brune was wandering the house in the dead of night. Following the light of the candle, Éliane tried to suppress the anxiety rising inside her chest. What if Lady didn't believe her? What if she thought Éliane had tried to enter the inner sanctum?

Her anxiety deepened when she found the door to Brune's room closed.

"I swear it was open just a few minutes ago," she whispered.

Lady gently pushed the handle to open the door, revealing a figure sleeping in Brune's bed. "You see? She's here."

"But she wasn't when I—"

"You must have imagined it, child," Lady said, closing the door before Éliane had a chance to enter and confirm it was indeed Brune in bed. "It happens. All the new sisters need a bit of time to get used to Sanctuary. This isn't an ordinary place, and you don't have an ordinary past."

A lump in her throat, Éliane nodded. She was so sure of what she had seen. Without adding a word, she went back to her room under Lady's gaze, who closed the door after whispering, "Good night, Éliane."

***

What an eerie dream, Éliane thought in the morning, until she remembered it wasn't. She *did* wake up in the middle of the night to pursue a shadowy figure she mistook for Brune, only to find Lady, who appeared next to her out of nowhere. The giant must have walked to Éliane without light—she could see in the dark, after all—and somehow lit the candle at the last moment, when Éliane was touching the door to the inner sanctum, as if she was about to trespass. How embarrassing! But the worst part was finding Brune in her bed, as if she had never left it. Did Sanctuary play tricks on her mind, Éliane wondered? Perhaps Lady was right. This was no ordinary place.

"Where's Brune?" Dulcetta asked as they found the dining table devoid of food. "She was supposed to cook breakfast today."

"I thought it was your turn," Carmélia said, to which Dulcetta answered by shaking her head.

As Éliane felt her heart clench with worry, Lady appeared from the kitchen with a platter of bread and jam. "Brune will be back in a couple of days," she said. "We're still running low on food supplies as Aralie took a good amount from the pantry for her journey, so Brune offered to travel to the village to trade gems against food."

Dulcetta's face went through a myriad of emotions. Éliane didn't have to look at the small shades appearing above the woman to recognize her feelings: confusion, worry.

"She shouldn't have," Dulcetta said. "We could have rationed the food."

Something in her voice told Éliane that Dulcetta didn't only disagree with Brune's decision but also questioned Lady's assertion. Éliane wanted to tell her about her night experience, but not in front of Lady. So she waited for the meal to be over and for Lady to leave for whatever activity she had planned for the day.

To Éliane's surprise, Lady left for the inner sanctum one more time.

It prompted Carmélia to say, "I hope she's not having another episode again."

Éliane let out a shaky breath. The more time she spent in Sanctuary, the more uncertain she became about the place's nature. It was supposed to be a refuge, but too many odd things had happened in a short period of time. Lady spending too much time in the inner sanctum was only one more.

"I must tell you something," she told Carmélia and Dulcetta, before telling them about the night's events. Esmée and Flavie were within earshot, cleaning up the kitchen. Éliane didn't mind them hearing the conversation. If something wrong was happening in Sanctuary, they deserved to know it too.

"Are you sure it was her?" Carmélia asked.

"I was until I saw her sleeping in her room," Éliane said.

Dulcetta stroked her chin. "Perhaps she left her room indeed and went back to it just before you and Lady went to check on her."

"That would be the most logical explanation, if it was her wandering the house in the first place," Carmélia said.

"If not her, then who?"

The question was from Esmée, who had stopped what she was doing to listen carefully to the conversation. All the sisters looked at each other, saying they all slept in their room and didn't wake up until the morning.

"Don't you find it odd?" Éliane continued. "I saw her walking to the inner sanctum, then this morning, Lady tells us she left to trade supplies at the village before any of us had a chance to see her?"

"I agree with Éliane," Esmée whispered.

"Brune would never go into the inner sanctum," Carmélia argued, her voice betraying her worry. She was obviously trying to reassure herself. "And you saw her sleeping in her room, Éliane. So she's obviously not down there."

"What if she is?" Esmée said, looking down and fidgeting with her fingers. "And what if Aralie is with her?"

Carmélia gasped. "What are you implying? That they never left, and Lady lied to us?"

"I-I don't know," Esmée said, visibly uncomfortable having such a tense conversation. "I haven't been in Sanctuary as long as you, but I've always found the inner sanctum... scary."

"And how so?" Carmélia said. "You've never been into it."

"That's why I find it scary," Esmée said. "Who knows what's in there?"

"Gems," Dulcetta said. "That's what's in it. We've all seen Lady come back with baskets filled with them."

"What if there's something *else*?" Éliane said. Esmée's worries echoed strangely with her own.

"It's forbidden for us to go," Carmélia said. "Why would Lady send Aralie and Brune into the inner sanctum if we're not supposed to enter it?"

"I don't know." It was Flavie. "But I heard something last night."

Everybody turned to the adolescent, casting apprehensive looks at her.

"What did you hear?" Éliane asked in a shaky voice. The more the conversation went, the more anxious she became.

"I thought it was part of my dream, but after hearing what happened to you, Éliane, I think it wasn't." She paused, as if gathering her thoughts. Then she continued, "It sounded like whispering coming from the walls, as if Sanctuary—the house itself—was *alive*."

"I heard the whispering too," Éliane said, the pressure inside her chest tightening. "Just before hearing the steps and following Brune's shadow."

"I've never heard anything like that," Carmélia said. "And I've been here for years."

Dulcetta nodded. "Me neither."

Éliane clenched her fists. Again, the thought that everything odd had started to happen after her arrival invaded her mind. She cleared her throat. It was time to share it with the sisters—hoping they wouldn't deem her *responsible*. "I swear I have nothing to do with Aralie or Brune's departure, or strange whispering in the walls... but I can't help but notice that it started a few days ago, after I arrived in Sanctuary. Is that correct, Carmélia, that things were fine before?"

Carmélia tilted her head. "Besides Lady's two episodes, yes. Everything was fine."

The four sisters stared at Éliane for a moment, their looks ranging from wariness to disbelief. At least none seemed angry or distrustful. *Not yet*, Éliane told herself, unable not to anticipate the sisters turning on her. She was a newcomer; someone they barely knew. If the High Seer had turned on Éliane, the sisters could, without doubt.

"Again, I swear I have nothing to do with what happened," she said, her hands quivering a little. "I'm just like you. A refugee." Perhaps it was time to be honest with the sisters. Fidgeting, she added, "I haven't been completely honest with you about my past, but fleeing someone who wants me dead is absolutely true. And they want me dead for no valid reason. I didn't do anything to harm them. I'm the innocent victim of someone who can't handle me being who I am and not who they want me to be, like all of you."

Dulcetta approached Éliane. Putting a hand on her shoulder, she said, "I trust you, Éliane. But tell us the truth now if you didn't before." She glanced at the other sisters. "We've all been honest with you. Whatever is going on in Sanctuary, we're in this together. We need to know."

Éliane nodded. "I haven't told you because I'm afraid she's still looking for me, and I didn't know if I could trust you not to tell her in case she found Sanctuary and asked about me."

"Who is 'she'?"

"The High Seer." Éliane took the pocket mirror she kept in her dress and removed one of her lenses. "I'm a seer from Aurië's temple. The one just a few days away. The High Seer wants me dead because she's jealous of my abilities. I had no choice but to flee. It would be her word against mine if I spoke up about her assassination attempt. I'm just an orphan girl recently turned seer. She's the highest temple authority."

One after the other, Carmélia, Dulcetta, Esmée, and Flavie approached Éliane and inspected her unconcealed pupil.

"She's telling the truth," Dulcetta said. "She's a seer. Those golden eyes don't lie."

"So you can see the future?" Flavie asked.

"She can glimpse at *possible* futures of people or places," Dulcetta corrected. Éliane nodded, relieved to be in the presence of another person familiar with Aurië and his disciples, so she wouldn't have to explain everything herself.

Carmélia put her hands on her hips. "This could help us. If you could... *glimpse* at Sanctuary's near future, you could check if Brune comes back with supplies. That would confirm she isn't in the inner sanctum."

"Or confirm our suspicions that she is," Esmée said.

Carmélia clicked her tongue, apparently still not ready to accept the possibility of Lady lying to them. Éliane didn't blame her. She had been in Sanctuary for a long time, building mutual trust with Lady.

"I'll do my best," Éliane said. She hadn't expected the conversation to take this turn, but it was for the best. The sisters didn't chastise her for coming to Sanctuary and had listened to her story without questioning it. "But I've never tried a glimpsing outside of the temple. It'll be harder without being on sun-blessed ground."

"Doing our best is all we can do," Dulcetta said. "All right, sisters. Let's not linger here. We all have work to do."

Chapter Twelve

The High Seer

What have I done?

The question haunted the High Seer, who awoke from another nightmare. Burning. She was burning in Aurië's light, punished for her vanity. She shook her head to chase away the memories of the terrifying dream. It wasn't only the nightly messages—these were sent by the Sun-God, the High Seer knew—that caused her remorse. Guilt seeped inside her mind night and day, reminding her of the terrible task she had given Shizelle.

What was I thinking?

Having the girl killed had seemed so easy. A simple solution to her simple problem. The High Seer wouldn't even have to spill her blood herself. Manipulating Éliane's friend to do it would work just fine. And worked it had. Only when the High Seer had seen the girl's dead eyes had she realized the utter reality of what she orchestrated.

She's gone, and I'll pay for it.

The High Seer didn't know if it was the desire to confront her own sin that pushed her to open the case in which she hid the eyes, but she regretted her action immediately. Not only did she cause Éliane's death, but she kept the proof of her demise as a token. How deranged was she to do such an awful thing? She had to get rid of the box, put it somewhere underground in the temple to give the girl a semblance of burial. Then she would pray Aurië for his forgiveness.

Contemplating the yellow eyes for one last time, the High Seer was about to close the box when an oddity caught her attention. One eye had partially turned brown. How could this happen? Seers' eyes remained yellow in death. The High Seer put gloves on and delicately picked the eye to observe it. Not only was the pupil turning brown, but its shape was slightly oval. The curve wasn't obvious enough to raise suspicions, but now that she looked at it closely, the High Seer doubted the eye's authenticity. If it wasn't Éliane's eyes, then who did they belong to? Or rather... *what*?

Did Shizelle lie to her?

A blend of anger and relief filled the High Seer's chest. Shizelle thought herself smart enough to disobey and fool her superior, which would normally require the highest penalty, but given the circumstances, the High Seer was glad the girl hadn't killed her friend. But if Éliane wasn't dead, then why did Aurië plague the High Seer with nightmares? He wouldn't need to punish her if no wrong had been done. Unless the girl had met a terrible fate after escaping. Wild beasts, bandits, Nunia's former disciples longing for vengeance—the threats surrounding the temple were endless.

What should I do? This question usually triggered a visit to the tower. If the High Seer needed counsel, Dame Héloïse was here. Except the matter at stake wasn't usual. How would the godkin react to the High Seer's confession? Would she help her fix the mess she had created or denounce her to She-Who-Sees-All? The High Seer exhaled. Dame Héloïse was wise. Much wiser than herself. Whatever she recommended, it could only make things better. If only she had listened to her in the first place and let Éliane accomplish this damn pilgrimage!

Furious at herself, the High Seer closed the box, tucked it under her arm, and dashed toward Dame Héloïse's tower. She found the door open and the godkin gazing at the horizon.

"I knew you would come sooner than later," she said, turning to face the High Seer.

"Do you know what I've done?"

Dame Héloïse shook her head. "I don't, but something tells me you are about to share it with me. I don't need to see shades to know how terrible you have been feeling since that little gifted seer of yours left for her pilgrimage. Sit."

The High Seer did as she was told and placed the box on her lap. "My apologies in advance for the gross sight, but I must show you."

Without further warning, she opened the box to reveal the eyes. She expected Dame Héloïse to wince, but only a furrowed brow and a curious look appeared on her face. The godkin picked an eye between her two delicate fingers and said, after examining it, "I don't know who tampered with these boar eyes, but they did a good job at making them look like a seer's." Then she looked the High Seer in the eye. "Isn't it intriguing that a wild pig's eyes are so close to our own? Of course, this raises the question: was it supposed to be the girl's eyes?"

Feeling her cheeks warm with embarrassment, the High Seer nodded. "It was. But I'm relieved by your assessment. It means she's still alive. Or was for some time, at least." Holding back tears of anger and shame, she confessed her plan to Dame Héloïse, without omitting the regrets and guilts she felt. "I don't know what to do. If Shizelle didn't kill her, then why am I punished?"

Dame Héloïse snorted. The old woman's pity for her was painfully obvious to the High Seer. "Regardless of Shizelle's success, your intent and the efforts you took to make it real are enough to deserve my father's ire."

Of course, the High Seer thought. She was punished not for the unknown consequences of her actions, but for said actions. "What can I do to redeem myself?" she asked, or rather, *begged*.

"Are you interested in redeeming yourself for the sole sake of your soul or because you truly care about the girl's fate?"

"Both," the High Seer answered. "To be truthful, I don't care much about her, but I still don't want her dead. Not really... I thought I wanted her dead, but I mostly wanted her *out of my way*."

"Because you thought she was a problem."

"She was. She still is. But the truth is that... I *am* the problem. Or rather, I *created* it."

Dame Héloïse cocked her head. "I wish I told you exactly these words when you came to me last time."

"Why didn't you?" the High Seer blurted, already regretting how her question seemed to put the blame on Dame Héloïse. "I mean, if I had listened to you, she would still be on her way to Fahein."

"True, but you would still be angry with her. My plan was to delay your actions. Use time to bring you back to your senses. I should have realized the urgency of your struggle. But enough with the *what ifs*. You asked me how you could redeem yourself. There is only one way. If this girl is still alive, you must find her. If she is in trouble, you must save her from it. And you must do it *yourself*. No more sending off pawns."

The words hit hard, but they hit right. It was *her* mess to clean. All she needed was to know where to begin her search.

"Don't think you will do it alone," the godkin added before the High Seer had a chance to answer. "Your regrets may be sincere, but I don't trust you not to have another change of heart. Also, I'm tired of this tower. I'm long overdue for an escapade. I'm coming with you."

***

Before finding Shizelle, the High Seer visited Seer Ahma in his office and announced her upcoming departure. "I don't know for how long I'll be gone. A few days, at best. Perhaps a few weeks. I need you to cover my duties in my absence. I'm granting you High Seer privileges until my return." She handed him an official letter signed by her hand, which he took in silence. She stopped short of telling him the nature of her absence, as now wasn't the time to deal with the outrage it would likely cause in the temple. First, she had to find the girl, or at least know what happened to her.

The High Seer found Shizelle practicing with another guard. They both stopped the exercise when the High Seer and Dame Héloïse entered the training hall. Shizelle held her spear upright, her fist clasping it with visible nervosity. She averted her gaze, defying the protocol that required her to look at her superiors, but her discomfort was so obvious that the High Seer couldn't hold it against her.

"Dismissed," she said to the other guard. Then, to Shizelle, "Follow me."

Shizelle didn't move at first. Was she scared for her life? Obviously she was, the High Seer thought, stifling the excuses she wanted to utter—this wasn't the place, and apologizing wasn't in her habits. Eventually, Dame Héloïse put a hand on the girl's shoulder and said, "You have nothing to worry about, Shizelle."

The godkin's presence seemed to reassure Shizelle, because she nodded and followed. Dame Héloïse rarely left her tower. She was a neutral, perhaps even comforting figure for the nuns and seers and guards living in the temple. *Thank Aurië she's helping me sort this mess*, the High Seer thought as she guided Shizelle to her office.

"You aren't in trouble," she told the girl after inviting her to sit. "If there's anyone in trouble, it's me."

Shizelle glanced at Dame Héloïse, who nodded to confirm the High Seer's words.

The High Seer pushed the box on the desk toward Shizelle and said, opening it, "I know these are boar eyes and not Éliane's." Shizelle gave her a panicked look, to which she answered, "I know it's going to sound strange, but I'm glad you didn't follow my orders. Don't make it a habit, though."

Shizelle looked down. "I couldn't do it. She's my best friend."

"Like the High Seer said," Dame Héloïse chimed in, "we are glad you did not kill your friend. What we need to know is what happened to her."

"Are you going to look for her?" Shizelle asked, a hint of bitterness in her voice. "So you can finish what I couldn't do?"

"No," the High Seer said. "We want to find her and, if she's still alive, bring her back to the temple."

"What your superior is trying to tell you is that she *regrets* asking you to kill Éliane. She should *not* have given you this order. She wants to repair her mistake."

"Is that true?" Shizelle sneered.

The High Seer exhaled. "I'm not asking for your forgiveness, Shizelle."

"Good," the girl muttered, a dark look on her face, "because I don't have any for you."

In normal circumstances, such a direct affront would have made the High Seer furious, but all she felt was a blend of shame and irritation. "Tell us what happened so we can find her. She's not safe out there if she left the pilgrimage trail."

"I will go with your superior," Dame Héloïse said, looking at the High Seer as if she was an unruly child, "to ensure she does the right thing."

The High Seer clicked her tongue but didn't say anything. Dame Héloïse treated her harshly, but it was justified. Godkins acted as counselors across temples of all deities for a reason. Still, the High Seer was growing tired of being reminded constantly of her failure. She was working on fixing her mistake. What else could she do? Castigating her wouldn't make Éliane reappear faster.

At least, Dame Héloïse's words proved themselves useful to soothe Shizelle to speak.

"Fine," she said. "I'll tell you everything."

***

According to Shizelle, Éliane had traveled east after their last encounter. She didn't share her destination with the girl, which complicated things, but surely other people had traveled the woods since then. Hunters, foragers, someone must have seen something. So instead of searching for a needle in a haystack, the High Seer and Dame Héloïse went to the closer village to the east, carefully following the road and sleeping in inns during the night. Even if the two women knew how to defend themselves—especially the godkin, who could burn her enemies alive with her light—tempting fate by straying away from the road or sleeping under the stars was ill advised. Nunia's followers still lurked in the shadows, and if her human disciples had lost their powers after the goddess's death, godkins had not. Like Dame Héloïse, they possessed abilities that caused serious harm.

After passing a few towns and hamlets in which nobody gave them useful information—at least their hunters had found no corpse in the woods, which was good news in itself—they reached the town of Norbury where they found their first lead. "There's a mansion up north in the mountain, about one day walking from here," a merchant told them. "I've never been, but I know a lad who goes every month to trade food with them. It's all women who live up there. Maybe your girl stopped in that place. Sanctuary, it's called."

They asked for precise directions, but the villagers either didn't know or didn't want to share. "They don't want to be found, those ladies, so you understand we can't tell you more."

"This is pointless," Dame Héloïse told the High Seer, who kept probing Norbury's folks relentlessly. "Come. We'll find it ourselves."

After four or five hours following a mountain trail north of Norbury, the High Seer was ready to give up what felt like an aimless hike when Dame Héloïse said, "I sense something. *Power*. A lot of it."

"Good or bad?" the High Seer asked.

"I don't know. This could come from this place. This ... *Sanctuary*. We should investigate."

The High Seer nodded and followed the godkin's lead. Dame Héloïse navigated the woods carefully, pulled by the power she felt deep within her bones.

"I still don't know if it's good or bad," she said as they found themselves on another trail. "I know it doesn't make sense, but it feels like both."

"How can something be both good and bad at the same time?" the High Seer asked, unsure of what Dame Héloïse meant.

"Believe me, it is absolutely possible," Dame Héloïse said, sneering. "You, first of all, should know it. But that's not what I meant, actually.

I feel *two* powers coming from the source. One is benevolent when the other is not."

The High Seer pouted but didn't respond to the taunting, focusing on the matter at stake. "Are you sure they both come from the same place?"

"Pretty certain, but we shall see when we find the source, should it be Sanctuary or something else."

After one more hour following the new trail, they reached a clearing where stood a mansion. Was it the place called Sanctuary, the High Seer wondered? She didn't have time to voice her question because Dame Héloïse said, an alarmed look on her face, "This is the place, but we shouldn't go. There's something terrible buried under that house."

The High Seer clicked her tongue. She couldn't feel anything like Dame Héloïse could. It didn't mean there was no threat, of course. "You said there's also something good here."

"Yes."

"Can you still sense it?"

"I can. But like I said, there's also something terrible."

"Any idea of what it could be?"

Dame Héloïse shook her head. "I am sensitive to other people's affinity with gods and goddesses. Especially with Aurië, but not only."

"Could this place harbor a godkin of Nunia?"

"Perhaps. But Nunia isn't the only malevolent deity," Dame Héloïse stated matter-of-factly—she knew the High Seer knew it. "It could be something else. Also... what I'm sensing is more powerful than a godkin."

"What's more powerful than a godkin?" the High Seer asked. A rhetorical question. She knew the answer, but couldn't believe it.

"A god."

The High Seer stood still, unable to speak. Was there a maleficent, dead god buried under this house? What was the benevolent power, then? "Do you think the person in this place is guarding it? To prevent people from awakening a malevolent god?"

"It would explain the benevolent force I feel. But now that I am closer, I feel something more ambiguous. I don't know if 'benevolent' is the right word. Regardless, I don't think we should go into that place. Wherever Sanctuary is, this isn't it."

The High Seer pinched her lip, unsure. "What if Éliane is there? We both know she may not be safe. If she's not, I must save her. You said it yourself."

"Even if it means risking your own life? You have an entire temple to care for. People need you. Don't be foolish."

"You mean 'don't be more foolish than you already are?'" the High Seer said, bitter. "If something happens to me, just tell Seer Ahma the temporary assignment has become permanent."

"Lysiane," Dame Héloïse pleaded, startling the High Seer. The last time she heard her name in someone else's mouth, it was on the day she became the temple's High Seer. Seer Lysiane had become the High Seer, leaving her personal identity behind to embrace her new function.

"I'll be fine," she said. "Stay behind and if something bad happens, come to my help or run away. Whatever is the best option in your opinion."

Dame Héloïse opened her mouth to argue, but before she could, the High Seer moved toward the mansion. The godkin muttered a curse but didn't follow, and instead hid behind a tree, watching. The snow cracked under the High Seer's feet as she progressed toward the entrance of the house. Observing her surroundings, she noticed how the snow stopped at the edge of the forest. She looked up. The sky was cloudy, but for some reason only the clouds above the house poured snow.

Dame Héloïse is right, she thought. *Something here is wrong.*

Still determined to check the place for Éliane, the High Seer walked to the door and knocked. Voices rose inside—all female, from what she heard—and the door opened at once, revealing an incredibly tall woman. She wore an amulet the High Seer recognized immediately. A round golden plate adorned with an olive branch. The woman was a disciple of Ido. A benevolent god. Was she the guardian of the evil thing lying under the house? At first, the woman had a soft face, but the moment she locked eyes with the High Seer, her look hardened.

"What do you want, *seer*?"

"My apologies for disturbing you," the High Seer said, uneasy. It wasn't the first time a stranger reacted negatively to her yellow eyes, but now wasn't the time to engage in hostilities. What concerned her, though, was why a disciple of Ido disliked her kind. To her knowledge, Ido had no quarrel with the Sun-God. "I'm looking for a place called Sanctuary."

"You've come to the wrong place."

The High Seer exhaled, disappointed, but not demotivated. The people living in this house could still know something. "I'm looking for a young woman from my temple."

"There's no seer here," the woman said tersely.

"Her name is Éliane," the High Seer continued. "She may not be here, but perhaps she passed by your place recently? I'm very worried for her well-being."

The woman raised an eyebrow, filling the High Seer with hope. Did she see the girl? Her hope quickly died when the woman said, "No. There's no seer living here, and I haven't seen any recently."

The High Seer remembered how Shizelle recommended Éliane to hide her nature. "She may not have told you. We have ways to hide our eyes."

This caused the woman to pause. But again, she replied negatively. "I'm sorry, but I can't help you." The woman moved to close the door, before adding, "Good luck with your search."

"If you hear anything or see her," the High Seer said very fast—a last ditch attempt to learn something, anything—"can you tell the people in Norbury? They know we're looking for her. Oh, and also, do you know where's the place called Sanctuary?"

"There's no sanctuary in these woods," was all the woman replied before closing the door to the High Seer's face.

Why such haste to get rid of her, the High Seer wondered? She knew folks living outside of villages liked their privacy, but the woman had displayed more than mere annoyance.

She sighed. She hadn't learned much, but at least she was well and alive. Dame Héloïse must have exaggerated her concerns.

"The woman living here is a disciple of Ido," she told the godkin after joining her back outside of the clearing.

"I still don't like this place," Dame Héloïse said. "I guess this isn't Sanctuary."

The Higher Seer shook her head. "It isn't, unless she lied. Remember how the people in Norbury said the women didn't want to be found? Anyway, I don't like it either. We can always come back later, better prepared. We should go back to the village for now. I don't want to sleep in the woods."

"Me neither," Dame Héloïse responded. Then, pointing at the sky above them, "Especially with that awful weather coming on us."

When the High Seer looked up, she gasped. Not only did the clouds turn almost black, threatening them with thunder, but another dark foggy substance hovered just above the mansion's roof. One Dame Héloïse couldn't see, for it wasn't a cloud.

It was a shade.

The largest the High Seer had ever seen.

Chapter Thirteen

ÉLIANE

Lady of Clairemont came back from the inner sanctum at the instant someone knocked on the door, before Carmélia could open it. Éliane didn't see who the visitor was, as she was busy carving gems with Dulcetta, and Lady sent the person away as quickly as she had rushed to the door.

"Yet another nosy person looking for someone who doesn't want to be found," Lady said during dinner.

"It happens sometimes," Dulcetta told Éliane, who glanced at her apprehensively. Was the nosy person someone looking for a sister?

To everyone's relief, Lady said, "Don't worry, it wasn't for one of you," but the inquisitive look she gave Éliane right after sent a shiver down her spine.

Did Lady lie? Had someone come from the temple for Éliane? This would mean the High Seer had discovered Shizelle's deception, which meant her friend was dead, which meant—*stop it*, Éliane told herself silently, exhaling to slow down her racing thoughts. Nobody came from the temple. Then why did Lady stare at her? Did the giant hear her earlier conversation with the sisters from the inner sanctum?

Thankfully, Lady stopped gazing at her and returned to her meal, giving Éliane a chance to observe the giant without being noticed. The other sisters often glanced at Lady too, their faces contorting in that blend of anxiety and curiosity Éliane was so familiar with. Not only were two sisters gone in unusual circumstances, Lady spent more time in the inner sanctum than usual, and she had sent away an unexpected visitor, but she also looked tense herself. As if the visit had shattered the façade of strength and control she always displayed. The brief shades appearing and disappearing around her were the proof of it. For the first time since the equinox, Éliane was able to see the negative emotions Lady hid deep within herself. And for the first time, she had a chance to identify a recurring one—not anger or sorrow or any of the emotions Éliane suspected.

A lanky shade sinuous like a snake.

Deceit.

***

Éliane sat cross-legged in her room, the door carefully locked, ready to attempt a glimpsing. The fresh memory of the deceit-shaped shade lingered on her mind. Who had Lady deceived? The unexpected visitor? Aralie? Brune? All the sisters? It was time to use her hard-earned abilities to learn Brune's fate, and perhaps put an end to her speculations. All she hoped to glimpse at was the sister back in Sanctuary with supplies, as Lady promised.

Alas, the glimpsing, so easy to her at the temple, didn't come. Éliane wasn't on sun-blessed ground and night had already fallen on Sanctuary. Without Aurië's light and sun-ale to help, any seer would struggle to glimpse at anything.

I can do it, Éliane thought, letting out a long sigh. *I'm good. So good the High Seer wants me dead. I just need a bit of help.* She moved to the window, looking for the moon. There it was, hanging in the sky and reflecting Aurië's light. It wasn't as good as direct sunlight, but better than total darkness. Staring at the moon, she recited the prayer to Aurië to attempt another glimpsing.

This time it came, but difficultly, as if something in the air prevented her from glimpsing. Was it the same thing that prevented her from seeing Lady's shades most of the time? But she persisted, and eventually her mind fell into a vision of oblivion.

All the sisters, dead, their bones buried deep underground. Sanctuary, bleeding darkness. Outside, night. Pitch-black night. Nunia's eternal night. Lady, standing in front of Sanctuary. Embracing the Night-Goddess herself who emerged from the mansion, her corporeal form unmistakable for a seer who had learned to know the enemy.

The vision faded, leaving Éliane breathless. Of all the possible futures she had glimpsed at, it was the most terrifying. *Possible, possible, possible*, she repeated in her mind like a mantra. *It's only a possible future. The most likely, but not ineluctable. It won't happen if I stop it.* And stop it, she must, because she had just witnessed the rebirth of a goddess. A goddess who slept under Sanctuary, Éliane realized. That's why Lady didn't want anybody to go into the inner sanctum. But Lady was a disciple of Ido! Why would she hide the dead Night-Goddess inside her shrine? It didn't make sense.

The answer floated in the sky, right before her eyes.

The moon. Or rather, *Aylinne the Moon-Goddess*, daughter of the earth and night. Lady of Clairemont wasn't a princess, or if she was, it was in a godly sense, as the daughter of Ido, the most powerful deity after Aurië. And if Ido was known for something, it was for his tumultuous affairs with all the gods and goddesses who would succumb to his charms, from Cyma to Nunia. Their liaison had given birth to the astral deity pulling the earth's oceans and ruling the night in her mother's absence.

Aylinne wasn't a malevolent goddess, according to what Éliane learned at the temple. She wasn't malevolent thanks to her father, but she wasn't benevolent either, because of her mother's influence. Whatever her nature was, Lady—no, *Aylinne*—planned something dreadful. Her motivations mattered little to Éliane, who was certain of one thing only: if her deductions were accurate, she had to warn the others, and she had to warn Carmélia first. If the pattern of disappearances continued logically—the sisters who had been in Sanctuary for the longest went missing first—then she was next. Éliane didn't know what role their deaths played in Nunia's rebirth, if the two were even connected or not, but something told her Carmélia was in danger.

Thankfully Carmélia's room was next to Éliane, so it took her only a few seconds to reach it. Holding her breath, she knocked on the door. No response. She knocked again, louder, while calling the sister's name. Perhaps Carmélia slept already. But nobody answered. She tried the door handle, which moved right away under Éliane's pressure. The door was unlocked. Inside, Carmélia's bed was empty. *Please, no*, Éliane pleaded silently, remembering the night she found Brune's bed empty. Maybe she wasn't in her room yet. It wasn't that late in the evening.

Carefully, Éliane went downstairs and looked for Carmélia in the shared areas of the house—the kitchen, the living room, the dining room. She even tried the small library in a corner of the house. The only person she found was Dulcetta, who was busy adding wood to the house's main hearth in the living room. She stopped what she was doing when she noticed Éliane's panicked face.

"Where's Carmélia?" Éliane asked precipitately.

"I don't know," Dulcetta said. "Probably in her room."

"No, she isn't. We need to find her now."

Dulcetta approached Éliane and said, putting a hand on her shoulder, "Are you okay? You look like a ghost."

"I glimpsed at a possible future," Éliane said before sharing her findings and deductions with the sister, who turned pale like a ghost, too. "She may be in the inner sanctum already."

"B-but we saw her at dinner just an hour ago," Dulcetta stuttered, visibly shocked by Éliane's explanations. "And how could Lady be the moon if she's up in the sky?"

"Gods can be in two places at the same time," Éliane said, her frustration growing. Now wasn't the time for a theology lecture. "How do you think godkins are conceived? Gods mingle among us in their corporeal forms without having to stop shining in the sky or do whatever they usually do."

Dulcetta didn't answer.

"I need to go down to the inner sanctum," Éliane said. "If I find Carmélia, or the other sisters... we'll know I'm right."

"And then what? We can't fight a goddess."

"We can't, but we can save ourselves and come back with people who can."

"Godkins?"

"Yes, though they're not as powerful as their parents. They could still do something." The ideal situation would be to find Aurië and warn him about Nunia's imminent rebirth, but Éliane would have to wait until morning to try summoning the deity. There was also no guarantee he would answer her call. Éliane needed to know *now*, and if the sisters were indeed in danger, to flee with them. "I need you to distract Aylinne while I go down there."

"She already went to her room."

"Then just watch her door. If she comes out, keep her distracted."

Before Dulcetta had a chance to answer, Éliane grabbed a lantern and walked to the inner sanctum's entrance. For a moment, she wished she was wrong and about to anger Ido for no reason. The Earth-God's anger, she could handle, but innocent women in danger? She didn't want to think about it. Being wrong would have been preferable to what she suspected. But if what a seer glimpsed at didn't always happen, the visions never lied.

Glancing over her shoulder apprehensively, Éliane seized the handle. Before opening the door, she looked at the glowing letters. *Down Lies the Heart of Sanctuary.* Was Nunia the heart of Sanctuary? Did Aylinne build the mansion above her mother's resting place to hide the dead goddess from everyone? Too many questions, and so little time for answers.

Gathering her courage, Éliane pressed the handle and entered the inner sanctum.

A steep flight of wooden stairs greeted her. Without a banister to hold on to and no light besides her lantern, Éliane carefully descended, one step after another. The darkness was suffocating. It wasn't the mere absence of light; it felt as if a cloud of obscurity pushed itself onto Éliane and her lantern, trying to extinguish the flame. Was Nunia truly dead? Did her rebirth already begin?

As she progressed toward the bottom of the stairs, whispers filled Éliane's ears. They reminded her of the ones she heard the night Brune disappeared. Nunia's voice? A dead goddess couldn't talk. Unless she was awakening already.

After a descent that felt like an eternity, Éliane reached even ground. The lantern barely emitted any light now. Feeling her way around, she moved slowly inside what appeared to be a large chamber whose walls were covered with stones. Éliane moved the lantern carefully, wary to extinguish the candle by moving it too quickly. The flame reflected its pale light on the stones, allowing Éliane to move by following the walls.

Eventually she found a door leading to another chamber. Shortly after she entered and closed the door behind her, a pleading voice called her name.

"Éliane? Is that you?" Carmélia's voice.

"It's me," Éliane whispered, as if she worried Aylinne could hear her. "Where are you?"

"In the cell."

A cell. So Carmélia was a prisoner, and the inner sanctum a jail. Why did Aylinne keep the sisters captive down here? To what purpose? Éliane let out a nervous sigh. It didn't matter why. Now wasn't the time to guess Aylinne's sinister motive. She had to free Carmélia.

Éliane walked in the direction of the voice, her lantern up, until metal bars appeared in front of her, and behind them, Carmélia's face.

"You were right," Carmélia said with a shaky voice. "Lady tricked me. She told me to listen to the whispers... then nothing. I don't remember coming here. All I remember is Lady pushing me into the cell and locking the door. Then she left."

"Where are the others?" Éliane asked pressingly.

"Aralie and Brune? I don't know. I didn't see them."

Maybe they are deeper in the inner sanctum, Éliane considered. But before searching for them, she had to help Carmélia. She moved the lantern to search for a key hanging on the walls.

"I heard a metallic sound in this direction when she left," Carmélia said, guiding Éliane. "If she left the keys down there, then it must be nearby."

After a few seconds of search that felt terribly long, the lantern shone a dim light on a set of large metallic keys. Éliane didn't know which one opened Carmélia's cell, but she was determined to try them all until the sister was free. Rushing back to the cell, she asked Carmélia to hold the lantern next to the lock so she could see what she was doing.

"The voice..." Carmélia murmured as Éliane tried one key after the other. "It's whispering again. Don't listen to it."

Éliane was too focused on the lock to pay attention to the whispering, but she still said, "It must be Nunia."

"The dead goddess?"

She nodded but didn't elaborate. She didn't have time to tell everything to Carmélia. Freedom first, explanations later. Finally, a key worked, and the cell door creaked open. "Quick, get out," Éliane told Carmélia, who didn't have to be told twice to leave her prison.

"Let's look for Aralie and Brune," the sister said pressingly. "Then let's get out of here."

Éliane found other cells in the room, but they were all empty. No sign of Aralie or Brune. "Maybe there's another door, another room with more cells," she muttered, mostly to herself. After a few minutes of searching for another exit, Éliane and Carmélia stopped looking.

Carmélia said the words Éliane couldn't pronounce. "They aren't here."

It could mean only two things. Either Aralie and Brune had never been into the inner sanctum, or they were still here. *But not above ground*, Éliane thought as she remembered the vision of the sisters' buried bones.

"Let's get out of here now," Éliane said, her chest feeling heavier than ever. "This place is not safe."

What she didn't say was how the lantern's oil level was dangerously low, threatening to plunge them into darkness at any moment. Taking Carmélia's hand, Éliane guided her toward the stone-filled room, but stopped when she noticed the door was open. She had closed it after entering the chamber.

Éliane was about to speak when a giant hand covered her mouth, muffling the scream that escaped her throat.

"Well," a voice said in the darkness—Lady, or rather, Aylinne. "The filthy little sun-gazer found her grave."

Chapter Fourteen

ÉLIANE

The lantern escaped from Éliane's hands and fell on the floor, shattering into a thousand pieces of broken glass. The burning oil spilled onto the floor, briefly revealing more of the surroundings before the flame vanished. Éliane still had enough time to see Aylinne hold Dulcetta firmly by one arm, preventing her from fleeing.

"I'm sorry," Dulcetta whispered in the darkness, to which Aylinne answered sharply, "Don't be, Dulce."

Carmélia let go of Éliane's hand and the sound of running steps echoed in the chamber. She was trying to escape. Another sound quickly followed—her desperate banger against the door. Closed and locked.

Éliane tried to free herself from Aylinne, but the goddess tightened her fierce grip and said, "If you make another move, I'll break your neck."

She didn't have the opportunity to try again because Aylinne dragged her and Dulcetta somewhere else in the chamber, while

Carmélia still tried to open the door unsuccessfully. Unable to see, Éliane's breathing quickened, adding to the dread her body and mind were already bathing in. She still felt the pain of being pushed to the ground and heard the door of a cell being locked behind her.

Trapped. She was trapped at the mercy of a goddess, deep underground where nobody could hear her scream for help. At least she wasn't alone in the cell. Dulcetta was next to Éliane, apologizing again and again for failing to keep Aylinne away from the inner sanctum.

"She knew," Dulcetta whispered, her voice interrupted by incontrollable sobs. "She felt your intrusion at the moment you entered."

"Of course I knew," Aylinne spat. "Why do you think I keep the door unlocked?" Without elaborating further, she moved away, her steps echoing in the chamber.

"Let me go!" a voice screamed—Carmélia. "I've done nothing wrong!"

"It's exactly why I need you," Aylinne said, before adding, "and why I need *all of you*, sisters. Only the soul of the innocents can feed the mother of night well enough to rise again."

So Aylinne was indeed trying to resurrect her mother, and feeding the sisters to the dead goddess was part of her plan. But why did it start after Éliane's arrival? Why did she keep the other sisters alive?

As if hearing her questioning, Carmélia said, with a pleading voice, "Why did you treat us so well for so long?"

"Because I needed seven of you at the same time," Aylinne answered, as if it was obvious. Then, her voice turning toward the cell where Éliane and Dulcetta were held captive, "If I knew a sun-gazer would be the last one to join..."

She pronounced the words *sun-gazer* with a poisonous voice, betraying her hate for Aurië's followers. It didn't surprise Éliane. Aurië had killed Nunia. Of course, her daughter despised the people who worshipped her mother's murderer. But Aurië didn't kill Nunia for no reason, Éliane wanted to tell Aylinne. It had been self-defense. Without light, all life on Ido would die. Nunia should have never tried to make night permanent by challenging the Sun-God.

What Éliane wondered, though, was when Aylinne found out about her nature of seer. Based on her wording, it sounded recent. Did Carmélia tell her? Or did Aylinne overhear her conversation with the sisters? What about the stranger who knocked on the door earlier? What if it was someone from the temple who asked her by name? But knowing the answer to this question didn't matter. It wouldn't change her predicament.

"Aylinne!" Éliane shouted, expecting that calling the goddess by her true name would shake her at least a little. "Your father won't let you bring her back." She didn't know if this was true, but hoped so. Ido had been Nunia's lover once, but it was before the goddess tried to engulf his realm in eternal darkness.

"Don't tell me what my father will or will not allow," Aylinne said, her voice unmoved and not interested in denying what Éliane had aptly guessed. "He knows I'm suffering. He does his best to protect me, but he can't keep me behind him all the time. I only have a few days per month of respite from the burning light of your abhorrent god. It must stop."

If Aylinne wasn't about to feed her to Nunia, Éliane would have felt sorry for the goddess. Who knew the sun's light hurt the moon? Everybody looked at the full moon in awe, when in reality the goddess burned and couldn't do anything about it. And it wasn't even her fault, Éliane supposed, and neither was it Aurië's. It simply *was*. It was unfair, but it couldn't change. At least, not by the means Aylinne planned. If Nunia came back, she would try killing Aurië once again, and if she won... no, Éliane couldn't allow the thought to take roots in her mind.

"You can't doom us all," Dulcetta argued.

Aylinne didn't respond, as if she preferred to ignore the consequences of her actions. Perhaps she didn't care. If Ido enjoyed the life growing on his body, astral deities usually didn't care about the lives of mortals. Even Ido might side with Aylinne. She was his daughter, after all. She was more important than the mortal life he fostered. Hadn't he interceded with Cyma in her favor, so clouds would shield Sanctuary from sunlight?

Then Carmélia gasped and said, "What are you doing?"

Éliane wished she could see what Aylinne did to Carmélia. Instead, she heard a thud, then the sound of something heavy being dragged.

"What did you do to her?" Éliane asked.

Aylinne's footsteps told her the goddess was moving closer to the cell. A flame appeared in the darkness, revealing Aylinne holding a candle. "For a seer, those pretty eyes of yours are quite useless now, right?" she sneered. Then she slipped her arm between the bars and grabbed Éliane head's, pulling her toward the candle. "Still hiding those yellow pupils, are you? How do you do it?"

The goddess's giant hand squeezed Éliane's skull painfully, but she still managed to say, her voice quivering, "L-lenses. We use lenses."

"Remove them," Aylinne ordered, letting go of Éliane's head.

Éliane shook uncontrollably. "I-I need a mirror."

"Don't make me do it," Aylinne answered, ignoring Éliane's request.

Taking a shaky breath, Éliane tried to calm her trembling hands. The thought of Aylinne putting her long fingers in her eyes to take the lenses out was enough to make her wince in anticipatory pain. Removing lenses required precision. Patience. Nothing Aylinne had at the moment. She would pick Éliane's eyes out, like Shizelle was supposed to do.

After several attempts, each more uncomfortable than the previous, Éliane finally removed one lens, then the other. She could barely see them in her hands. She tossed them to the ground and looked at Aylinne. If she was as brave as Shizelle, she would have given the goddess a defiant look, but the only thing her eyes were capable of was shedding tears. Tears of utter fear.

"I wish I could stare at him without hurting," Aylinne said bitterly while she stared at Éliane's yellow pupils.

Then she lit more candles, allowing Éliane and Dulcetta to see Carmélia's body lying on the ground. Next to her was an empty syringe. What did Aylinne inject her with?

"It's time for Carmélia to join Aralie and Brune," Aylinne said, answering Éliane's unvoiced question by pointing at the ground. The two sisters were buried to feed the waking goddess.

"What did you do to them?" Dulcetta asked, pressing her face between two bars. "Where are they?"

"They're dead," Éliane whispered, lowering her gaze. "I'm sorry, Dulce. She killed them."

"No, no, no," was all Dulcetta managed to say. Looking at Aylinne, she added, "You swore to protect us!"

"I swore to protect you against the evil you fled," Aylinne said. "Which I did. I didn't promise anything else."

"You're a monster," Dulcetta said, shaking the bars of the cell. "Let us go!"

Aylinne ignored her. She grabbed a shovel lying on the floor and started digging. "I did not expect to do this tonight," she said. "Our sun-gazing friend is forcing my hand. Don't worry, you will join her sooner than later. Then Esmée and Flavia will follow, and my work will be done."

Éliane let out a scream of despair as she thought about the two sisters still above ground, totally ignorant of the disaster happening in the inner sanctum and of their impending doom. If only she had a way to warn them, to tell them to flee and seek help at Aurië's temple. Dame Héloïse could do something. Not kill the goddess—only a god could kill another—but her light would surely be enough to chase Aylinne long enough to save all the surviving sisters and stop Nunia's rebirth.

As Aylinne kept digging, ignoring Éliane and Dulcetta's pleas, Carmélia began to move again. Whatever Aylinne had injected in her body didn't work anymore. Did she only paralyze Carmélia? Did she plan on burying her alive? This made sense if Nunia was to feed on her. This made sense, but did not make it any less horrific.

Crawling away from Aylinne with great difficulty, Carmélia moaned in pain. Aylinne muttered a curse and threw the shovel away before rushing to the sister.

"Leave her alone!" Éliane screamed, to no avail.

Aylinne caught Carmélia by her neck, then lifted her in the air as if she was a doll. "Please, don't make it harder. You wouldn't want to be conscious down there, would you?" Closing her hands around Carmélia's throat, she started suffocating her.

Make it stop make it stop make it stop. The words kept repeating themselves in Éliane's mind like an endless prayer. Even if she voiced her wish, no one would come to make it happen. Not Aurië. Not Ido. Not Dame Héloïse. They were alone, facing a goddess determined to kill them.

"You don't have to do this," she said, anger rising inside her chest as she watched Aylinne strangle the poor Carmélia, who had gone limp again already. "Why are you choosing to be a monster like your mother?"

"I have no choice," Aylinne said, her voice booming in the chamber. "I have suffered enough. It's your turn now, sun-gazer."

Éliane grabbed the bars and said, her voice louder, harsher, "Take me, but leave them alone! I'm your enemy. Not Carmélia, not the other sisters."

"Seven innocents is all it takes," Aylinne hummed, "for the mother of night to finally wake. Seven and not one less."

This was pointless. Aylinne wouldn't change course. She had already sacrificed two sisters. What were five more in her grand scheme of things? Mortal lives didn't matter to the gods, but they mattered to Éliane, who was one of them. She had known the sisters for only a few days, yet their lives were still dear to her. Even if she had only met them this morning, she wouldn't stand by while Aylinne murdered them.

Fury rose inside Éliane's chest, slowly but surely chasing the fear away. Her eyes now used to the dimness, she glared at Aylinne as if her seer's eyes could pierce her flesh. How dared she? How dared she welcome all these women with open arms, house them, feed them, protect them, only to bury them alive when the time came? All Aylinne did was raise them like cattle, readying them for the slaughter. Nurturing their innocent souls with promises of shelter, of a better life away from the people who wanted them dead. She was like the High Seer, who had welcomed her to the temple to better orchestrate her murder once Éliane's presence became too cumbersome. Except the High Seer didn't plan on dooming all life by doing so. Both Aylinne and the High Seer acted out of selfishness, but Aylinne was willing to let millions perish to achieve her goal.

"Enough," she muttered between her teeth, feeling her body warm up with anger. "I said enough, Aylinne!"

As Éliane shook the bars, desperately trying to break them with the little strength she had, Dulcetta gasped behind her.

"Éliane!" the sister shouted. "You're burning!"

Éliane stopped staring at Aylinne for a second to look at her own body. She wasn't warming up because of anger only. She was literally burning, a cloud of light and flames emanating from her body. What in heavens was going on?

"Too hot," Dulcetta said, pressing herself against the wall of the cell, as far as possible from Éliane. "What are you doing? You're going to burn us all!"

"I'm-I'm not doing anything," she said, as the flames rose and the light became more intense, illuminating the chamber.

Aylinne dropped Carmélia and stared at Éliane, fear appearing on her own face for the first time. "How? How did anyone let a godkin become a sun-gazer?" she asked, her voice a blend of disgust and anger with a hint of panic.

Nothing and everything made sense at the same time. Éliane was a seer, and she was a good one because her body wasn't that of a mere human. The unknown father who had abandoned her mother before Éliane was born was a god. The one she now served as a seer, when she should have become a counselor like Dame Héloïse. How could she not know? Hundreds of questions raced through her mind, about her mother, her family, the orphanage, the temple, the seers, Dame Héloïse...

Questions she didn't have the luxury of time to answer. In front of her was Aylinne, a goddess she thought she had no chance to beat as a human. A goddess she could now rival as a child of Aurië. No matter why or how she was a godkin, now was her chance to fend off Aylinne and save the sisters. Drawing her ire from inside her body and mind, Éliane let the flames grow and the light shine. The cells' bars melted under her touch, creating an opening, an opportunity to rush toward Aylinne and save Carmélia—which Éliane did as soon as enough bars were gone.

"Leave Carmélia alone!" she shouted, pushing Aylinne toward the opposite wall. "Let us go!"

Aylinne screamed in terrible pain when Éliane grabbed her arms and moved her away from Carmélia and Dulcetta, so she could amplify her inner light without hurting the sisters. The goddess shrieked and curled up into a ball, trying to make herself smaller than she was. Éliane's light was a fragment of Aurië's, but it was enough to hurt the Moon-Goddess. She still struggled to believe Aurië was her father, and for a moment wondered if the light and heat were something else, but Éliane's memories of Dame Héloïse using her own light during the summer solstice rituals told her they were the same. She had stopped wondering who her father was many years ago, but now she was happy to have an answer. An answer that could hurt the goddess in front of her.

It's now or never, Éliane thought, ready to wrap Aylinne in a veil of unbearable heat. She leaned over the goddess and pushed all the light at her, unleashing her inner fury. Aylinne screamed and screamed until her voice faded. The light was so intense, blinding, that Éliane couldn't see a thing. It's only when she took a step back that she realized the goddess's corporeal body had turned into a pile of unrecognizable ashes.

"She's gone," Éliane said in disbelief.

The goddess wasn't dead, Éliane knew, but she had repelled her earthly incarnation, giving the sisters a chance to flee. Quickly turning to Carmélia, she saw Dulcetta leaning over her, trying to wake her up.

She approached them, but Dulcetta shielded Carmélia with her body and said, "Don't come closer, Éliane. You're still burning!"

Éliane stepped back, scared. She didn't know how to stop the light.

It wasn't the only problem she had. The chamber had caught fire where Aylinne stood before vanishing into nothingness. If they didn't leave now, they would suffocate before dying in a burning inferno.

Rushing to the exit, Éliane pressed her hands against the locked door, burning an opening through the wood. "We need to go," she told Dulcetta. "Can Carmélia walk?"

Dulcetta gave a distraught took to Éliane. "I don't think she's still alive, Éliane."

"No," Éliane said, as if denying Carmélia's death would bring the woman back to her feet. "She's just unconscious. Aylinne didn't mean to kill her, not before burying her."

Dulcetta shook her head. "She's not breathing, and her heart doesn't beat anymore." She moved Carmélia's head to show her throat where Aylinne had pressed her giant thumbs. Nausea rose inside Éliane's throat as she saw the blueish marks covering Carmélia's skin. Dulcetta was right. Carmélia's chances of surviving such a long and brutal strangulation were non-existent.

Éliane fought back the tears coming again to her eyes. "We need to go. Now."

Dulcetta nodded, but instead of rising and following Éliane, she said, "We can't leave her here. She has family."

She wanted to carry her body to the surface, Éliane realized. With so many steps to climb, how could Dulcetta carry Carmélia's weight? Dulcetta was a strong woman, but not strong enough to carry someone. Éliane had to calm her light so she could help carry Carmélia. Anger had triggered it. Serenity would likely extinguish it.

But how could she be serene in such a place, surrounded by death and fire?

Slowly, she inhaled and exhaled. *Aylinne is gone. We're safe now. Dulcetta and I will go back up, warn Esmée and Flavie, then we'll leave this dreadful place forever.* The reassuring words worked enough to reduce her light to a gleam. She carefully approached Dulcetta, asking her how hot she felt. After the sister confirmed it was bearable, Éliane helped Dulcetta lift Carmélia's body and together, they climbed the stairs, leaving the inner sanctum and the shadow of Nunia behind them.

***

It still snowed when Éliane, Dulcetta, Esmée, and Flavie walked outside of the house. They stood and watched the flames rise in the sky, melting the white blanket covering the clearing.

Sanctuary burned.

And above, in the sky, the moon shone brighter than ever.

Epilogue

SHIZELLE

You, a godkin?

Nobody knew, not even Dame Héloïse, yet you found your nature at the right time. Should you have found it before, Aylinne would have felt it. She would have never let you enter Sanctuary. Another poor soul would have found its way there instead of you. The seven sisters would be dead, and Nunia, alive and well. By becoming the seventh sister yourself, you stopped the rebirth of a calamity. What about the High Seer? Her egoism led you to Sanctuary, saving us all in the end. A mere consolation considering how wicked her motivations were, even if she changed her mind after the deed was allegedly accomplished.

She was half-way back to Norbury when Dame Héloïse stopped her, explaining she had just felt a godkin appearing out of nowhere. One like her. A half-sibling, though you have become a full-fledged sister to her now. They rushed back to Sanctuary, following the light of the giant fire that was consuming it. They found you and the three other surviving sisters next to the inferno, crying over the corpse of a fifth woman, comforting each other. The High Seer was smart enough to let Dame Héloïse approach first, so you didn't run away. You didn't know about the High Seer's change of heart, and even if you did, you wouldn't have believed it.

You didn't tell Dame Héloïse what happened. You didn't tell her anything because you couldn't speak. Dulcetta spoke instead, telling Dame Héloïse about you and Aylinne and Nunia. Even for an old godkin like Dame Héloïse, it was too much to absorb, so instead she invited you and the sisters to follow her back to Norbury, and the next day, to the temple. You remained silent on the way back, barely looking at the High Seer. She looked at you, a blend of relief and shame gleaming in her eyes, but she was, once again, smart enough not to speak to you. You weren't ready for an apology.

When you crossed the threshold of the temple's gates, I cried. You cried too, when I hugged you. You had worried about my fate for so long, as much as I worried about yours. I thought my sister was dead, yet you came back alive, more powerful than ever, and with more sisters to join our family. You wished you could have saved them all, but you did your best, and nobody expected you to save people nobody knew were in danger until it was too late.

The High Seer back, Seer Ahma was supposed to step down from his temporary assignment, but he didn't. The High Seer preferred to leave her position and join She-Who-Sees-All, what she had tried so hard to avoid. Her own actions had sealed her fate. At least she would bring knowledge of Nunia's attempted resurrection and help She-Who-Sees-All prepare for another attempt, should Aylinne come back. Not a terrible fate for a woman who plotted her subordinate's death. Her efforts to repair her mistake didn't go unnoticed, even if they felt, to you, too little too late.

The sisters? You saved them from Aylinne, but they still feared their former persecutors. Seer Ahma, the new High Seer, agreed to give them sanctuary—a real one, this time—as long as they needed. In exchange, he wanted their insights on Aylinne, so he could prepare for her next attempt to bring back her mother. Will they stay? Only the future can tell. Some may choose to stay at the temple, while others may leave and try putting their lives back together. Regardless of their decision, they have a new family they can count on. The temple's doors will always be opened for them. As for the poor Carmélia, her body was sent back to her family in Valenmont with a letter detailing her life in Sanctuary and how the surviving sisters missed her. Aralie and Brune got proper funerals, though it felt unfair to do in the absence of their bodies. Digging in the ruins of Sanctuary was too dangerous. Nunia's body was still there, somewhere deep into the ground, and the High Seer preferred to leave it undisturbed for now.

Then there was you. The seer-godkin. Never in centuries of choosing nuns at the orphanage had the temple mistakenly turned a godkin into a seer. What were the odds for a child of Aurië to be abandoned? None, people believed, because a woman birthing a godkin was blessed by the gods themselves. Even if it happened out of wedlock, nobody would blame her because she birthed the child of a god, making a family proud for generations to come. Why did your mother hide who your father was, preventing you from growing up with a loving family? Only she knew, and she was long dead. What mattered was to know what to do with you now. Would you follow Dame Héloïse's path? Or remain a regular seer, with the quirk of being able to burn houses down? You didn't know, but you had time to choose.

For now, all you cared about was being back in the temple.

Being back home.

Being back with me.
Your first sister.

Acknowledgments

I cannot open acknowledgments without thanking my spouse Félix for his unending support—and for helping me fix this manuscript and the massive plot hole present in the first draft. Thank you, thank you, thank you.

My publisher Tony Anuci comes next, for trusting me not only with one book, but two. You are a pleasure to work with, and I am fortunate to be published with Anuci Press. Working with the press to help make this book a reality are also Adrian Medina, who designed the perfect cover, and Robert Ottone, whose insightful edits helped this manuscript shine. Thank you both!

I also want to thank all the people supporting my writing career, even if they were not involved directly in the making of this book. Their presence anchors me every day, ensuring I have the energy to write, edit, and promote my books. My agent A.J. Van Belle and my wonderful agent siblings; my writer friends Florence Chien, Morgan Wodring, Linda Stewart, L.N. Holmes; the Book Inkers;

the #SmallPitch and the Bonaparte Dynamite folks; and many, many more. Thank you for being here.

And to you, reader, for reading this book. You are the reason I keep writing. Thank you.

About the Author

Millie Abecassis is an author of fantasy, fairytale retellings, science fiction, and horror from France. She is a graduate of the Panthéon-Sorbonne University and now works in the biotech industry. When she isn't reading or writing, you can find her playing video games or in her backyard trying to stop her wisterias from taking over the world. Millie lives in San Jose, California with her spouse, their cats, and too many plants to care for. You can learn more about her writing and other endeavors at www.millieabecassis.com. (Photo: Clayton J. Mitchell)

www.ingramcontent.com/pod-product-compliance
Lightning Source LLC
LaVergne TN
LVHW020446070526
838199LV00063B/4860